CW01086414

DISTORTION

SIERRA ERNESTO XAVIER

Grosvenor House
Publishing Limited

This book is published by
Grosvenor House Publishing Ltd
Link House
140 The Broadway, Tolworth, Surrey, KT6 7HT.
www.grosvenorhousepublishing.co.uk

This book is a work of fiction. Any resemblance to
people or events, past or present, is purely coincidental.

A CIP record for this book
is available from the British Library

Paperback ISBN 978-1-80381-494-0
Hardback ISBN 978-1-80381-495-7
eBook ISBN 978-1-80381-496-4

INTRODUCTION

This is a book about the forming of a relationship despite immense difficulties. It is also about how we become aware of the role of our bodies in everyday life: our relation to our and other people's bodies. The manifestations of histories, memories, emotional and psychological states are laid out in terms of the physical, including distance and space, as the two characters unravel their story.

Yet, despite all this, I chose not to take the easy path of using descriptions to inform the reader. I made a stylistic choice to use dialogue only. Something which is unusual but not unheard of (see Manuel Puig's *Kiss of the Spider Woman*, works by Nathalie Sarraute and, to a lesser extent, Noah Cicero's *Human War*). The outcome for the reader is that they can only experience the point of view of the characters.

Imagine, if you will, that you are having a conversation with your partner, your child or a close friend regarding intimate or personal issues. You are there, listening to them with the occasional awareness of how they sit, position themselves or what they may be wearing. But this awareness is for a brief moment before you return to the conversation with someone who is in need. You are with them, yet not fully observing them because your focus is on *what* they are saying. The 'what' helps you understand and support them. There is a journey of discovery and of piecing together their landscape of emotions, psychology and history so that, out of respect for the other, you can comprehend, empathise or sympathise based on what they reveal.

As the reader becomes more involved with the dialogue, they will become part of a discovery journey, piecing together the two character's stories. You are within and no longer observing a scene or setting.

The dialogue will reveal to you what the characters look like, their memories, thoughts, ideas, and, just like talking to a close friend, the reader will ascertain their motivations from what is being said. Readers, understandably, want the environmental descriptions, the actions and motivations so that they can journey with the characters. But the journey here is the dialogue itself: the journey is not absent, it is there, only in a different format; the dialogue is the landscape.

This book is also minimalist in design. It is neither an operatic nor an epic work. It is a set piece where we discover some physical descriptions of the characters and their environment, but it rests there. The journey begins at point A and ends at point B, but we do not know at which chronological point it begins. Therefore, it is not supposed to anchor the reader to some point in time or place, but to anchor them to the dialogue, as if listening to a loved one. The intimacy of their dialogue becomes the intimacy of their setting – confined and seemingly unconfined. The exteriority is minimal so as not to distract from the dialogue, which in turn emphasises the human body in this story.

I hope the reader will see *Distortion* as a different kind of venture from a writer in development.

Sierra Ernesto Xavier.

DISTORTION

In a Bed

You are beautiful without your clothes on. Your naked body makes me feel wonderful. I like it when you are here lying next to me, when I can run my finger gently down the length of your spine, along this scar that you have.

I like it when you touch this scar of mine. I can feel your finger travel from the back of my neck down to my arse. I love the feel of it. Do it one more time for me.

It seems so peaceful and so serene. It tells me that there is much pain, much horror.

It feels nice. It feels as if I am being opened up, as if a knife is slowly tearing me apart.

Do you like pain?

It's not about pain. It's about the possibilities – how things might once have been. I can only imagine the beauty of it all ... But your finger makes it all seem possible again, makes it all beautiful. You should know you have the power to make me feel that way. To remind me of the things that could be.

But it's painful for me to know that you can be so beautiful and to know the horrors that you must have endured ... Does my finger cut you open?

It's a pleasure – to know that you are next to me: turning me on with your fleeting touch, cutting me apart. It makes me feel alive. It makes me feel like a woman and not like some kind of deformity.

There is nothing wrong with you, my love. You are perfect.

You cannot say that. Can you not see the meandering river, that scar where my tears have flowed and which your finger has now brushed aside?

I do not see the tears. I see the beauty of your back in all its nakedness. Such horrors do not bother me, such tears I do not see.

There have been tears … many tears, all of which have run down that river.

I believe it. But when I am with you, I do not see the river meandering.

And when I am with you, I feel that there are no bends in that river. It becomes a dry river where there are no tears. I am happy, I feel beautiful and all the possibilities of the world are not needed. They are not needed when you are here, when your finger runs down that river, down my spine.

When you are with me you do not need those possibilities, but I think that you still wish they were real.

My heart wishes, because of the way you make me feel, that for you this river should have no bends, that the river shouldn't have this deformity.

I love the "S" shape of your spine. Your scoliosis does not bother me. When I look at you I do not see any deformity. I see a river that runs straight.

4

Do you see the pain, my love?

I see tragedy.

That's why I like you: it's because you understand. You understand what it means to know the tragedy of it.

Yes, you seem to be stuck in wanting the river to run straight and believing it meanders.

Is it not there for you to see when you run your finger along my spine?

I see beauty … and a woman who believes she is not beautiful.

I feel beautiful. I _am_ beautiful when I am with you.

When you are with me? You are beautiful always.

How can you say that? How can you say that the river runs straight when I am lying here like this? Can you not see the rock formations, how tall they are? Can you not see the unevenness?

You are beautiful without your clothes on. I like it when you are here next to me like this.

Cut me, cut me once more! Show me how to be happy!

Here … my finger … along this horror …

Do you feel it? Do you feel the peaks next to this river?

I feel nothing of the sort.

You feel it, I know you feel it. My shoulder-blade – it juts out …

When I touch you, there are no peaks … there is no unevenness, only a woman who is beautiful.

It is a price of failure – the failure to achieve what is possible, to achieve … normality.

As I am here, you are normal.

As I am here, I am a deformity.

You mustn't say that word. You promised.

I'm trying. I'm trying to like the beauty you see. These are only our first few steps. But you must tell me the truth. The truth about what you see. The truth about what you touch. The truth about what you feel. That is the only way.

You are beautiful and I am happy you are here. You may want me to cut you open but I want you to be as you are.

Your finger … it is about the surgery, the trauma of things going wrong … about how, in my mind, it could have been so different … Run your finger down my spine … run it around the peaks … run it around the boulders.

There are no boulders.

There are! Can you not see?! They are there … under that peak, can you not feel them? Even the river seeks to avoid them, to avoid the harshness of the landscape.

When I look at you, I see nothing other than you.

Do you see the S-shaped curve of my spine?

I see it. I see the curve. I see your right shoulder blade, higher than the other, protruding. I see the hump of a rib just below, with scars across it. But when I am with you … here, and elsewhere … I see only you the woman.

See, you do see the ribs, those boulders that burst above the land and give me that hump. Do you not think I am hideous?

It is I who am hideous, not you.

You are hideous because you see me as normal.

I am hideous for other reasons and you know what they are.

No, my love, you are not hideous. You are beautiful … Here, let me turn around … I want to see you. I want to see your naked body just as you have seen mine.

Keep your lower half covered with the sheet. And keep me covered too.

There! We are safe now.

…

What do you see when you look at me?

I see a handsome man.

There is no beauty in my face.

There is beauty … all over … <u>especially</u> in your face.

How can you say that? How can you say that when I can barely look at you when you are looking at me?

This nakedness is as difficult for me as it is for you.

Hide me. Hide my face, my love. Quick! Give me your hand. Let me place it over my face.

Oh, darling … let me see.

No. We agreed – one step at a time. I need this.

Be brave, my love.

How can I be brave? Do you not see the gorges, the ravines and crevices?

They are hiding behind my hand. Let me see … let me see the beauty of it.

No. Wait … There is too much pain, too much trauma cascading over the rapids. My tears will come.

I am here. We are here. We agreed to look at one another, to touch when we feel comfortable to do so. You have seen my horror. I need to see your pain.

Let me move your hand slowly. Let me be the one to move this cloud from over my face. Let me do it slowly … What do you see?

I see perfection.

You see … an abomination.

I see a handsome man.

You make me want to cry … to know, having wished for so long … that someone, somewhere could even like me.

Oh, darling! This tear that you cry … let me kiss it. Let me kiss it as it runs down your cheek, let me envelop your tear with my lips.

You kissed me! … My face. You kissed this aberration.

I kissed you.

No one, *no one* has ever done that. How could you have wanted to touch this hideousness with your lips?

I see no hideousness, just beauty.

Don't, please don't. Your words are hurting me.

Come here my love. Let me hold you in my arms. I am here for you.

…

There is so much pain inside.

I can feel it in your body as I hold you.

My body … it remembers. It remembers everything.

Does it know you are mine?

It knows that I am ugly.

You are beautiful.

How can you say that? How can you say that when you look at me? Tell me what you see. Tell me the truth. You promised. You promised honesty. Can honesty and beauty exist together?

Let me look at you.

I want to remain here, in your arms.

To hide?

Yes … to hide.

Let me see the truth of your face. Let me see, as we have agreed.

…

I can see you now. I can see the truth.

Is the truth beautiful?

I see a man ashamed. A man locked in wanting, and knowing the possibility is not there … a man who cannot lift his head.

It is the past. It is crippling me.

I am here.

What do you see? Tell me what you see.

I see the same man as I saw yesterday … and the day before … and the day before that.

Describe what you see. You never tell me what you see. Do you see the slopes and the rocks where the tears have flowed?

I see the contours of a perfect face.

No, no, you mustn't. How can we move on if you cannot tell me the truth? Give me your hand. Give me your finger … Here, what do you feel?

I feel a perfect mesa, a perfect forehead.

Do you see where the mesa has crumbled, where it has subsided, eroded?

I see your right eye – angled, slanting.

Angled? Yes, where the subsidence is. Do you see where the debris is, where the boulder has fallen?

I see your right eye, slightly larger than the other.

Do you see the slippage of the earth?

I see your cheek.

Do you see the aftermath, the escarpment that it has created?

I see your right cheek sloping to one side, paralysed.

Such natural disasters!

Nature is beautiful.

And here … what do you feel?

The tenderness of your lips.

No … tell me … what do you see?

I see … a lip, scarred … turned up on one side.

Remember – the truth… everything.

I see your lip –

Torn!

Scarred.

Pulled up.

Raised.

Yes, raised. Where is it raised?

Darling.

You must.

… The right side of your upper lip is raised to the level of your nostril.

Is nature beautiful?

You are, my dear.

How can you say that? Do you not see the cavern it exposes?

I see the teeth that your lip can no longer hide.

Do you see the crevice?

I see a scar.

You see the crevice, as if a knife had torn it, cutting me apart.

I see a scar that has healed.

Do you see horror?

I see suffering.

It has tightened, pulling my lip upwards.

Let me kiss you, my love.

No, you mustn't! ... Tell me, what else do you see? Do you see the ridge?

I see your nose ...

Describe the lie of the ridge to me.

It bends to your left.

Do you see the precipice?

I see your nose, my love.

And the steep face on the right side of the ridge?

I see a man whose cartilage is missing.

You see the collapse of features, a complete collapse of my nose on my right side.

I see nothing but you, my love.

Can you see ... my nostril ... this one, on the right ... being pulled up by the apex of the crevice beside it, and that as my nose, and its tip, bends to the left, it has elongated that nostril, collapsing it?

I see something that is natural and beautiful. I see a man whom I love.

Natural? ... Nature ... Mother Nature ... Mothers can be so cruel.

...

Do you see the hurt, my love?

I see tragedy.

You knew I would understand your tragedy.

I also see pity.

You see deformity ... the ugliness of it all.

I see you, my love, nothing else. Just as you see me and not the S-shaped curve of my back.

I find it difficult ... difficult to look at you ... to even raise my head to look at you ... You are beautiful. I am not.

I see a naked face, the soft tender skin of a naked face. Natural. Faultless.

How can you say that? How can you –

I like it when you are here next to me without your clothes on.

Hide me. Hide me again. Show me the way to the possibilities. Show me the way to being with a woman, to being with you. Cover my face, take away the hurt ... even if only for the duration of a shallow breath.

Let me lie back again; this time I'll be on my back, facing you ... Let me see your face from where I am ... Do not hide the way you feel.

...

Touch me, touch my body ... touch this landscape that confronts you, feel the harshness of the country.

I see beautiful hills and valleys.

You see harshness – a landscape spoiled.

I see a landscape beautiful.

Touch me. Let me take away your hurt.

I can't.

Give me your hand, my love ... feel the ruined identity in front of you ... feel the poverty.

I see no poverty. I see richness, an unspoilt landscape, a beautiful woman lying next to me.

Here, let me take your hand.

Wait … Let me do it. Let me touch you.

Remember … the truth.

I see a sight that could be framed. A landscape that could have been painted.

No … please … please. You promised.

What I see is what I feel.

Why are you so reticent?

I am not. After what you have described of me, I see nothing but perfection in you.

Spoilt landscapes are not perfect. I am not perfect. There is only perfection in truth, and as I have given you the truth you must tell me what you see and not what you feel.

Yes, I know … it must be both ways.

We must know the land we live in. Give me your hand … Let me guide you.

No – let me do it. I need to do this. I need to do this at my pace.

Look at me, then.

You know I find that difficult at the moment. You know that I am trying … Let me look at this land of yours … I have never seen anything so wonderful.

What do you see?

I see perfect skin.

What do you see <u>here</u>?

I see … your collarbones, your neckline.

Describe it to me.

I see an uneven neckline, higher on the right than the left.

I am not perfect.

You, my love, have nothing wrong with you.

Yes, I do … Look below, look below … describe what you see.

I see … your breasts.

Touch me. Touch me, my love.

I can't. I am afraid. You know me. I fear myself: I fear drowning in my feelings.

Don't be afraid … feel me.

No, my love. We agreed – one step at a time.

What do you see, then?

I see a wonderful woman.

No. What do you <u>see</u>? Describe my breasts.

I see your left breast, which is slightly larger and lower than the right, pushed forward by the curvature of your spine.

Do you see the sunken land? Do you see the harshness of it?

I see … a small chest cavity on your right side.

Do you see where my right breast has sunk … hiding… recessed in the cavity?

Yes, I see your breasts. They are beautiful.

Touch me, touch my sternum, feel the edge of the cavity.

I feel it.

Then how can you say it is beautiful?

To me, you are.

No, no. Can you not feel the hard edge of the cavity?

All I feel and see is your femininity.

You are so sweet, my love.

It is something I am afraid of. Your sexuality overwhelms me.

One step at a time, my love.

You have such a beautiful stomach.

Your hand upon my stomach makes me feel wonderful, makes me want to cry. It is the only perfect part of me.

You are perfect all over.

That's what I like about you: you are so nice.

Your stomach is so nice.

Describe more of what you see. Tell me what you see, tell me the truth about this landscape. Can you see the fault in the earth's crust?

I see a woman who excites me.

Do you see my hips? ... Here, let me pull the sheet down slightly.

Yes ... I do ... wonderful.

Do you see the mountain?

I see no such thing.

You see where the tectonic plates have collided, where the bony hip rises above the land?

I see the loveliness of your left hip.

A hip that juts out.

Something that adds character to your landscape.

And the other side?

The other side is equally beautiful to me.

Describe it to me, darling.

It is as flat as your stomach.

And?

And … it is lower down your body than on the left side.

Horror at the back. Horror at the front.

Woman from the back. Woman from the front.

I wish you could cut me open here. I wish you could give me the possibilities … by running your finger along my neckline, tearing me apart down the middle of my body, cutting along my uneven hip-line.

Your body does not need any more trauma.

It needs to be alive.

I am here.

You keep me alive whilst my body wants to forget. It wants to forget the tears, to alleviate the hunger. Such hunger, such poverty, so obscene.

Your land is fertile. It has so much of value.

23

Do you value its harshness?

I value everything about you.

Even my sex?

I'm trying. You know that I have difficulty there. I really am not ready to see it yet.

I know. I am sorry. I am sorry to have said anything, to have made you anxious … Lie down. Lie back. Let me view your landscape, this country of yours. Let me see it as you have seen me.

…

Keep the sheet covering me down there …

I will.

What do you see, my love?

I see a beautiful plain.

Truth, my love – can you see the truth? Can you see where the body remembers? Run your fingers along its memory.

You are beautiful without your clothes on. Your naked body makes me feel nice. I like it when you are here lying next to me, when I can run my fingers along these furrows, these scars.

You finger reminds me of –

Of the possibilities?

No … of all the failures … of all the pain.

My darling, am I hurting you?

No, my love, you are not hurting me. But what do you see? What do you see when you see all those furrows?

I see a landscape that is beautiful, a landscape that has been tortured.

Is torture beautiful?

Torture is never beautiful. But your body is, to me. And within that body I see torture … I see hurt all over this body – it is a tortured beauty, and one that I am grateful for.

Are you grateful that I have been tortured?

I am grateful for your survival.

Describe what you see. Describe the torture you see.

I see furrows –

You see scars.

I see a scar, here, on this side, one that runs along a rib. I see another running along a rib on your left side.

Further down ... what do you see further down?

My finger… it runs down the centre of your body, down the smooth, flat lands of your body … to your navel.

And beyond the navel? What is down there beyond the navel?

A beautiful plain.

Look at the sides of the plain, at the sides of my waist, where you are at now.

What have they done to you?!

What can you see? Can you see the hurt?

Here … on your right … I see marks of torture, a furrow running along the crest of your hip. Wait; I see another furrow on the crest of your left hip.

Torture here, Torture there!

I see scars that excite me.

Does my hurt excite you?

Your body excites me.

Look at me … give me your hand … cover my face, conceal me in the dark.

No. No more hiding. No more running away.

When I face you, and then turn my head the opposite way from you to the other side, what do you see?

I see the side of your handsome face.

Look closer. Look at my ear. What do you see?

I see … nothing.

Pull my ear back… see the hidden treasure …? Can you see it?

I see … I see another furrow, another scar, curved, behind your ear.

And now when I look up what do you see?

I see scars across your columella, the part of your nose that stems from your upper lip to the tip of your nose, separating your nostrils.

Do you see how handsome it all is?

I see how handsome you are.

Now that you have seen me, how can you want a body with such pain?

I see a body with much to offer. I see a body full of character and a man ashamed of his past, a man unable to see that another body craves his.

You are beautiful. I am not.

My body tells me everything. It tells me it wants you.

Truth is always distorted.

Our bodies are the truth.

Against a Wall

I like it when we sit here side by side against this wall. Even though we only have this sheet to cover our waists, it allows me to see the contours of your secret. It makes me feel excited. I can only imagine what the sheet is hiding from me.

I also like the contours of your body, especially the way the sheet moulds itself around your sex.

Can I put my hand under the sheet and touch your sex?

No, not yet. I am not ready and am somewhat scared.

Won't you speak to me about it, my love?

I can't.

Talk to me, let me hear your pain; whisper if you have to, it will be easier.

It's not that I don't want to …

Please, my love. I am here.

I know you are. But there are things in my past that make me remain *there*. Things happened there, in my past.

What happened?

Things that are difficult to speak of.

Can we go there?

No. Not yet.

Let me know when you feel okay to go there.

It's good that you feel comfortable with your sexuality.

It was not always so. Like you, there are things in my past, also. Perhaps we met there.

What do you know about the past?

I know that it can eat you. That it can tear you apart.

A beautiful person like you! You know nothing!

I know pain.

Yes, I can see it.

We all have pain – all of us. It doesn't matter how little it might seem to others; to the individual it is immense.

Nobody wants someone with baggage.

I want you.

You want sex.

I need you.

You need someone to have sex with.

That's unfair!

Life is unfair!

It is what you make of it.

The past is unfair.

Is that where you are now – in the past? ... Be here, with me.

Of course I want to be here with you. But I want to hear your pain. Did you like it there – in your past?

Sometimes it is best left there.

Tell me what happened there, in the past. I need to know. I need to know why your sex smells wonderful.

Why don't you look at it?

Perhaps, soon.

Soon is in the future. Your past will be there also, if you cannot let go of it.

I know … you see … I still hear the laughter. Can you hear it?

No.

It is there, in the past. And it is here with me now. It echoes inside me, reverberating through my body.

No one is laughing at you now.

They are, in here – in my head.

Why are they laughing?

Let's not go there just yet. The past is better left there, as you say.

What about the trauma all over your body?

It's similar to yours, I suppose.

The past is present here physically on your body. What does your body remember?

The memories are there for everyone to see – exposing me without my consent.

It's a terrible feeling, your privacy being invaded.

Yes, it is like your most personal and private part is constantly on display, exposed to everyone – a violation.

I feel like my legs are spread out in a medieval stocks for all to see what should be private to me, but my clothes hang different and I walk differently – everyone can see it. It's like their eyes are all over you, inseparable from your body.

You are right. There is no difference between their piercing gaze and our bodies.

Is that why you are afraid?

My own torture, private torture, the scars, the furrows, for all to know.

Tell me about your torture. My body needs to know that it is not alone in its suffering.

Do you delight in my suffering?

My body feels delight in knowing that pain does not occur to me in isolation, that the isolation is crumbling, knowing that there is this collective horror between you and I, that there is comfort to be found with the pain of others.

Have you been in that space – the space between help and torture – that "Other Space"?

Yes. Yes, I have. It is a horror that no one will understand.

What do you understand it to be?

The helplessness. The paralysis. Screaming and shouting inside your head.

That Space where you are nothing, where you are ignored.

Yes, like in life.

No one sees us.

Like photos other people take with us in them which seem to disappear from their collections when they show their family and friends.

Erasing us from their lives.

As if we do not exist or that they are ashamed of us.

Being in that Space, we were helpless because of their actions. Paralysed by their audacity.

What a nightmare to be there.

To be awake in a sleeping body.

Trapped, encapsulated, inside your own cage. My body, my cage.

My face, my cage.

One's pain, one's suffering.

There and not there.

Mine started with the injection – it left me in that Space.

That needle … you could feel it pressing down on your skin, causing your skin to be tense around that area. Then there is that moment of pain when it pierces the skin, the metallic sharpness is pushed into you. And when you think that it is all over, they show no mercy, they give you no time to object as they press the plunger and you feel the coldness of the anaesthetic rolling into your veins, feel the chill move up through your arms, devouring your blood as it spreads, pushing itself forward, like water finding its way up a tube when it is being siphoned. Because you are aware of it, you consciously follow this chill that is infiltrating you. Suddenly ... suddenly, you feel the coldness inside the blood vessels around your brain, consuming it ... And then, then ... your eyes close. They close without you willing it, as if something is forcing you to be asleep and only leaving you time enough to acknowledge the last moments of consciousness. No more sound to be heard, no more sensations to be felt: left at the mercy of others. Your body in suspension.

How could I forget!

Then, there you are ... you become awake inside your body, aware of everything, and those masks are ready to operate.

I was aware of it all: the incisions, the stretching, the tearing, the hammering, the chiselling.

No one hearing our screams or our shouts. Just the torture being inflicted.

Imagine being locked in that Space, helplessly witnessing your landscape being altered.

I know. I know.

Yes, you understand tragedy.

Your torture, it fascinates me, it intrigues me. Talk to me, tell me about it.

They made incision after incision, cut after cut, knife after knife and they did not think to inform me before they did this because they did not want to … frighten me. They treated me like a child. They saw my face and thought I was not worthy of respect. A *tabula rasa* – that's what I was to them.

What did they do?

It started here, in my right eye. Hidden furrows that you do not know about … You see this escarpment on my right side: my cheek somewhat paralysed? They started by pulling my lower right eyelid down so that they could expose the inside of my eyelid. I am not talking about the eyeball itself, but where the soft red and white of the inside of the eyelid meets the eyeball. They pulled the lower eyelid down from the outside and held it in place with a two-pronged hook to keep it open. Then they brought a knife to my eye, cutting me just below the eyeball, from one side of the eye to the other, opening a wound to see what was underneath my eye, my eyeball now connected only to a small cuff-like section of that red and white softness that had been freed from the bottom flap, which remained connected to my lower eyelid.

Next, they used a pair of tweezers and lifted this small, rim-like section attached to the lower part of my eyeball upward over my eye, suturing it to my upper eyelid. It was like someone cutting your abdomen and pulling the skin over your head.

They peeled back the lower cut and used some sort of spatula to separate the skin from the muscle and then the muscle from the fat on my bone. It felt like someone ripping parts of my body apart with a blunt instrument.

As I lay there, people peered into my body, gazing no longer at my face but inside my face – nothing left for me to protect!

They pulled the underlying fat upwards, just like someone pulling a blanket when you are sitting on it, forcing your body to move towards them. This is how they lifted my cheek – by pulling on the fat and then tying it, securing it, stitching it into place. Restoring me to what they thought was normal. The scar hidden, no trace for others to see.

That's when they told me that the bone that surrounds my eye was ... irregular.

What does that mean?

It was slightly smaller and more angled than it should have been, on the underside of my eye. That's why my eye looks like a fallen boulder.

No, it doesn't, my love.

Truth! Remember, the truth!

It doesn't. It is nothing like a boulder.

The operation was supposed to make me look as if my cheek had not fallen down my face ... and it did for a while.

But why operate inside your eye?

Your cheek and eyes muscles become accessible from that part of your face. Better there than slicing through your cheek.

They want to hide everything!

Over time, my cheek did not want to be there. It wanted to be back where it had been, and as you can see, it pulled down the outer corner of my eye with it.

Another time, when I had breathing problems, they said they could solve that, too. They took me and they tried to suffocate me, whilst they thought I was asleep. They stuffed packs of absorbent material up my left nostril, forcing it in. I wanted to move my head backwards because of the force they were using and to stop them suffocating me, but my head wouldn't move – I was paralysed by the anaesthetic. You cannot imagine how much they packed in – one forceful movement after another, like someone trying to choke you by ramming things down your throat. They did the same to the other side, so I couldn't breathe through my nose.

They were suffocating you.

Then the knife came out and they started to cut me. They hid the cut again so that they could leave no evidence of what they were going to do.

Where did they cut you?

From here, the columella. Only it was done from the inside wall of my nose just adjacent to that point. They started there, dragging their knife upwards cutting me to the underside of the tip of my nose and then all the way around the inside of my nostril. First one side then the other.

Can you imagine someone tearing you apart like that?

They peeled the lining of my nose away from the cartilage, muscle and soft tissue, leaving me vulnerable to their instruments. Another knife was used to cut away the side of my septum – the bony part of the nose that separates the left from the right. They took out small pieces of cartilage, scraping it, cutting it from either side, and chopped and shaped them into small battens which they then shoved straight back in, only higher up towards the tip of my nose, where the elongated pieces were pushed into and along the ridge of my nose. They said it was to widen my nasal airways by making my nose broader. The irony was that I was suffocating from what they had rammed into my nose before they started.

Another time, another two times, they promised me that things would improve. Another two times they came with their weapons and in one fell swoop slashed me here, across the columella – and this time they did not try to hide it. On two different occasions they scythed me, ripping me open, and when they realised that they had left evidence of these cuts for all to see, they went into the inside of my nose and followed their previous cuts.

Once they had done this, they inserted the lower arm of a large, L-shaped implement into my nostrils as far as it could go and pushed forward the other upright arm of the L, to lever it over my head. I could feel the coldness of the implement pressing on the floor of my nasal passage, whilst their levering lifted and ripped my nasal tip from my bone, leaving the blood-red septum naked to all, exposing my internal nasal passages, as if I had no nose, as if it had been gnawed or cut away in some kind of barbaric act – a raw, exposed piece of bone with some flesh and blood. All I could picture was me walking around like that!

If that was not enough, another team worked on another part of my body at the same time. I lay there being assaulted simultaneously on both occasions. People taking bits of my body away from me: cutting, beating, bashing, shaping it, as if it was Plasticine. I could not imagine that any of them gave any thought to me and my body integrity at that time.

These two rib scars, here, are where they incised into my rib muscle using a scalpel, creating a wound with two flaps, one on either side of the cut. They opened me up, peeling the muscle flaps apart. Then came another knife – a "flesh" blade – to cut along the thin covering that was over my ribs and which sat under the muscle. They peeled this covering apart and inserted yet another instrument in me – it looked like a miniature hand-held sickle, something that helps farm the land. The only difference was that the curved hook was at right angles to the handle, bending downwards. They used the curved end to bluntly scoop their way around my rib, following its contours, and strip the underside of my rib away from the thin, flesh-like covering that surrounded it. Then, almost as if parts of me were a toy, they placed the blades of some heavy-duty cutting shears above and below my rib, and by squeezing the handles of the shears together, the blades cracked through my rib, snapping it, first at one end and then the other. Then they removed the pruned piece from my body, from where it belonged, and played with it like Plasticine, shaping it to suit their endeavours.

What did they do with the Plasticine?

Whilst they pivoted my nasal tip as far back as possible, with their L-shaped implement, they now wanted to build up my septum, the very thing that they had destroyed previously, to provide support to what they had done before and then to increase the projection of my nose.

By way of all these nightmare cuts and slashes, they continued and continued, trying to correct me to make me more acceptable. Not once did they think about me – I was their experiment. When it did not go right, they wanted to do more. And they did more: these two scars here, behind my ears, they have their own stories to tell.

As if destroying my ribs to get cartilage for their sculpting wasn't sufficient, they attacked my ears, removing the cartilage from the back to help build up further parts of my nose to increase the air passages to help me breathe easier. This nostril here has hidden in it some of my ear cartilage. It was meant to prevent the collapse of my nostril and to widen the nasal passage. The saddest thing here is that they had to do this because the scar tissue from their previous work was causing the problem. They attacked me on two separate occasions when I lay on their table so they could perfect my landscape.

None of them saw that the scar from the original cleft lip repair was shrinking from an already shortened lip, that not enough lip existed to keep it aesthetically pleasing, that their second attempt had resulted in making my appearance worse – a scar shrinking and thus opening up a huge crevice.

One after the other they kept performing on me. Not one of them thought of looking at me in my totality; all of them wanted to deal with their own experiment, to focus on their own singular issues.

Shh! Enough, enough for now, my love ... You rest – let me speak instead. Let me tell you what they did to me.

They started on me by turning me over onto my front, once they thought I was asleep. They got a knife and placed it at the top of my spine, at the back of my neck. They pressed the knife into my skin, piercing it – I felt the pain of the incision. The pain ran through me like a bolt of lightning, through my head and into my teeth. They moved their knife all the way down my back, following the curved river that I have there, slicing me open.

As they moved the knife down my spine, I could feel the leading edge tearing into my skin and I could feel the pain that lingered in the exposed rip that it left in its trail. My body wept with blood as I craved to arch my back with the pain of it all.

Then, and I don't know what implement they used, they scraped back the layers of muscle, ligaments and other tissue to expose my spine. I could feel every tenderness, every fibre being ripped, being evicted, as they did that.

Then … then the burning sensation – as they cauterized me where they had wreaked their havoc, to stop the bleeding. First, they ripped me, then they burned me.

They held apart the two soft sides of the incision – clasping the skin, the muscles, everything. It seemed like they cut me open and pulled me apart so easily, exposing the inner cavern so that they could consider the next steps of their torture.

Somewhere at the top of my spine, below my neck, they took a hook and screwed it into the bony spikes of my spine. I could feel the gnawing at my bone as it was slowly driven in. Each turn of the screw's thread was burrowing its way further into the bone. It continued and continued, for what seemed an epoch, rocking my spine side to side as it was screwed in.

It was such a relief when they stopped. It left the hook sitting on top of the bone and the screw-like thread buried inside the bone, trying to make it look like it was a part of me.

Those bastards!

And before I could catch my breath, they did it again, only this time to the lower vertebrae above my pelvis on the same side of my spine, driving the hook into the bone. I could feel the vibrations run down my legs.

Then they inserted a metal rod, connecting the two hooks together, securing it to the hooks so that it would not fall out. The rod was straight and attached to the top and bottom of the S of my spine. The tips of the S were connected. Their instruments were now in place.

Next ... there was a jolt in my back. Something was moving me in my paralysis. The jolt occurred again and I realised what was happening: the rod was ratcheted, and each time they slowly turned it, it would move the hooks further apart, the upper hook moving further upwards and taking with it my spine. They were stretching me, elongating my spine, crank by crank, to reduce the bend in my spine – trying to make my S look like an I.

I lay there in front of them, my body offering no resistance whilst they mechanically altered it. A long metal rod held the two ends of my spine apart, stretching it out like on a medieval rack. And just to show the world what they had done and to make the change permanent, they screwed hooks into the same vertebrae but on the other side of my spine, so that they could reinforce the structure by placing another rod parallel with the first. I was now being stretched by two rods either side of my spine, and to ensure the longevity of their work they reinforced the rods with horizontal support struts between the two at several points, thus ensuring that this "exoskeleton" was rigid and sound. I was now their human cyborg.

Why? Why do they inflict such horrors, such brutality upon us?!

It is to correct what life has given us.

Brutality in life, brutality in correcting life.

Once they stopped, they resected the rib on my hump, for cosmetic purposes, but mainly, like they did on you, to use it elsewhere, to use the bone to fuse my spinal vertebrae, so that I could have more stability in my spine. It was when they scraped the surface of my vertebrae, to bleed it and expose the inside, that they slapped on the malleable bone from my rib hump in between my vertebrae, to try and fuse the bone. Once finished, they decided to conceal their torture by closing me up again, sewing and stapling me back together.

My god! We are born to suffer!

I needed the rod to support my spine, but later you could see the shape of their construction under my skin.

But I did not see anything emerging from under your skin.

I know you didn't. That's the tragedy of it all – to have a glimpse of a straight back for a few weeks, and then for it to be all gone.

How?

The past is very painful sometimes. Physically painful ... My whole back was on fire, swollen, throbbing. The slightest of movements and my body was enraptured with the sharpest of pains shooting along my nerves. I was a wreck, crying physically, emotionally and spiritually. They had to sedate me. And even then, I could feel the pain.

This happened after my operation, after they put me on a bed and strapped me down on it so that I would not move. They put what seemed to me to be some kind of framework on top of me, from my toes to my head. There was a little gap for my face, so that I could breathe, but they had full control over me.

They rotated the bed so that I was upside down, facing the floor, the framework preventing my body dropping to the ground. They said it was to relieve the pressure on my spine. I could still feel the pain, though. It would not go.

Over the next few days, the pain increased, so much so that it was unbearable. My back began to swell up, my temperature was high, I was in tears. They pumped me full of drugs, which they put directly into my veins, but the pain remained. I wanted to rip out my own back because it was so painful.

I remember it affecting my whole body, and at one time I had no control over any part of my body: whilst in that prone position I humiliated myself – I wet myself and my urine flowed onto the floor. The pain and the embarrassment were so great that I cried and pleaded, and eventually I went under the knife again, this time to remove their contraption.

I had an infection from the bone fusion, that destroyed some parts of my spine.

All that torture, all for nothing.

What have we done, for the world to inflict so much pain on us?

We have done nothing!

...

Come, let me put my arms around you.

As I said, some things are best left in the past.

Then why do you want me to talk about it?

Because I don't think you ever have.

It's best to distance yourself from it.

Some people can. Others carry the weight of it, like you.

Perhaps.

You still haven't told me about these two scars on either hip.

...

The same thing was done to both sides, after they had scalpelled their way into my hip bone: they held the two sides of the cut wide open to expose my hip. They hacked all the way around the crest of the hip, using a hammer and chisel. I could feel the force of the hammer jolting through the chisel and cracking my bone; it felt like a machete hacking into me.

When they had hacked all around completing a circle, they just lifted the crest off, like a lid – simply lifted off. Not only were they looking inside my body, but they were looking inside my bones – and I wasn't even dead yet.

Then they would use a gouge or a spoon to scoop out the bone from inside the hip, so that they could molest it and use their artifice elsewhere.

Where did they use it?

One time, they tried to build the right side of my nose, the bit where it meets your cheeks, and also lower down, where it forms the foundations that your nostrils sit upon. They wanted to even out the appearance of my face, despite the huge escarpment on one side. They cut inside my mouth, where the cheeks meet the gums, and shoved their artifice into the small opening they had created, fixing it to the part of the cheekbone where it meets your nose, hiding once again what they were doing by cutting me where no one could see.

47

You must have been screaming and shouting, and all unheard because of the paralysis.

And they continued, time after time, despite me telling them to stop.

They hear you then they ignore you.

Just like the photos: they see you then they want to erase you.

We were pieces of work to them – the next on the production line.

Like all the others, they left a mark on me, too.

But why did you go through so many operations, especially if you were aware of everything?

That's the question I keep asking myself. Perhaps I did not want to be lonely in life and then to die a lonely death.

I had real problems: there was movement in my face; the grafts would slowly shrink, unsettling what was done; the scar tissue would not heal or allow things to remain as they had intended.

I know what you mean: we had to be disfigured to correct our disfigurement, only for it to leave us further disfigured.

My god! What have our parents done to us, for us to endure this?!

We brutally disrupted their happiness, their hopes, their aspirations … their futures.

By not being perfect.

Rudely forcing them to accept that they had to love us.

Yes, shaking their façades when they showed their children to others.

Destroying their happiness.

Disrupting their ideal lives.

We are so brutal!

And they condemn us to our bodies.

Brutally disrupting our normality.

Condemning us to corrections – to living this brutal life.

Yes – to living it. But what happened with the bone they took from the other hip?

…

Are you all right?

Yes.

You seem a bit distant.

Sometimes, as you say, the past is best left there.

There is nothing so awful that, between us, we have not gone through and survived.

...

They used hooks and clamps to keep my mouth open as wide as possible. Contraptions that stretched me wide, pulling back my upper lip as far back as possible towards my forehead, to drag my mouth even wider.

They took a sharp blade and brought it into my mouth and placed it above my left molar, the rear-most tooth on the left, halfway between the root of the tooth and the place where my gums meet my cheeks. They pressed down on it and pierced my gum, cutting right through, dragging the blade all the way round my upper jaw to the other side. They were tearing me apart again.

They forced a spatula into the incision and moved it up and down all the way around my upper jaw, so that they could make the cut wider and loosen the gum from the bone.

They got another instrument and inserted it under the cut gum line that formed a skirt just below where my cheeks met my gums, and then they lifted my upper lip further back. I could feel it coming away from the bone. They kept pulling so much that they exposed the bone of my upper jaw and also my nasal passage. Imagine that – seeing the bone structure of your nasal passages from inside your mouth because they had pulled your face back so far, exposing your eyes!

As if that torture was not enough, I could hear some kind of electric saw approach me. And even though my body was paralysed, it caused terror in me. The anticipation of what was going to happen almost killed me. The rotating saw entered my mouth, first embedding itself on the right side of my upper jaw, above the cut line of my gums. I could hear and feel the vibrations as it cut into my jaw. It was so loud, because it was near my ear.

They moved the saw all the way around my jaw, from right to left, over the base of my nasal passage.

No!

There was nothing I could do.

Next … *next* … they got a chisel and placed it at the base of the septum, where it attaches to my upper jaw. All I could feel was hammering – they were chiselling away at my nose to separate it from my jaw. Hammer blow after hammer blow.

How could they do that!?

Then, I remember, I remember thinking it was over.

During what seemed an eternity, it felt like they were going to assault me again. I wanted to cry, but I could not.

There they were – two forceps. Coming towards me. Then someone standing behind my head, inserting one arm of one forceps in my left nasal passage, resting it on the upper side of my jaw, above the roof of my mouth. They closed the other arm inside my mouth, curving it around my teeth and resting it on the roof of my mouth, clasping my upper jaw between the two prongs. They did the same with the other forceps on the other side of my nose, ensuring that my jaw was clenched. When I felt the second forceps clamp me, you would not believe how frightened I was. You would not believe the panic that ran through me.

The person behind my head had grasped the two forceps, both of which were clamping me through my nose and my mouth, and with two or three quick thrusts backwards with his hands he cracked open my upper jaw, forcing it forward so that it separated from my skull.

I could hear the crack. It was loud. What could I do? I was in the hands of torturers. At that moment, I realised that my jaw had been left hanging, swinging in mid-air, with just the soft tissue in my mouth, the back of my palate, holding it in place.

It must have been a breathtaking and magnificent sight – to see a part of your body seemingly floating separately from you.

They moved my jaw forwards so that my top teeth were now in front of my bottom teeth, allowing me to bite food properly. It should have also somehow lessened my "sunken-faced" look, but it did not, it just moved my jaw forward. My face remains gaunt.

No, my love, it does not.

They used small L-shaped bone plates to re-join my jaw to my skull, drilling and then screwing one arm of the L plate into my skull and the other into my jaw to fixate the jaw, ensuring that the bone would fuse together by putting in place the bone graft that they took from around my hip fracture.

Then they pulled my dress down.

Your dress?

Yes, my upper lip, which they had pulled over my face just so that they could have a good look. Once they did the deed, they could pull it down, sewing me up after to conceal the evidence of their torture.

I was the face of their newly discovered Joseph Merrick.

And I was the torso of their Joseph Merrick.

It's terrible of us to refer to him like that. He had it much worse than us.

Yes, I know – but they tell us to look at people much worse off so that we can put things into perspective. It never helps, though.

They say it to shut us out; they don't want to hear about us.

Because they can't deal with it themselves, so why should they deal with us?

They alienate us and hide us away psychologically. It's a way to erase us from their minds.

Erase us, so that our offensive nature is not inside their minds.

They don't want us inside their minds or in their personal photos – since photos are like memories.

We may not be in personal photos, but we are certainly consigned to medical photos.

We become specimens, something to look at … objectively.

They stripped us of our dignity, photograph after photograph – turning us into mere curiosities.

My face was photographed from all angles in all its evolving states, no matter what level of hideousness they thought I was at. Pictures of my face, before, during and after their torture – whilst it was being ripped apart, whilst it was being cut – to demonstrate the bone structures of what constitutes an oddity. They said it was for medical reasons. To use in training for future medics – but it was a victory cup for the surgeons, to pat themselves on the back for their discoveries.

For my part, my breasts, my body was exposed for all to see: frontal photos, side photos – first the left side then the right; close-ups of my sunken breast, my angular neckline and my uneven hips. Then the final humiliation of the rear photo – of how I am curved, crooked, my deformity revealed – photos of me with just my knickers on. All this and only my eyes redacted – as if then you could not tell it was me!

It was all done to humiliate us: to record our disfigurement so everyone could laugh, so that future generations could laugh; for us to be humiliated for eternity in their books.

And yet we are lost amongst all those photographs. For the sake of research, we are exposed, stripped naked, casualties of our already reviled bodies. Our humanity is violated, stripped and lost forever in medical photos.

Their collections, when displayed, are like a circus of photographs, a freak show.

To be raped of our dignity, to be raped of our integrity, to be raped of our respect. How can society violate us so much?

On the Floor

What are you doing?

Lying on the floor.

I can see that, but why?

I need to talk to you

On the floor?

Yes, come and be beside me … curl up next to me … your back against mine.

Together, in isolation, in this open space.

Cover yourself with this sheet that is draped over my waist.

…

You're bony …

Don't you like me?

It's not that. I wasn't criticising you.

I know you weren't.

It's just that I have never been back to back, skin on skin with anyone. So I'm noticing things for the first time.

It's all right.

It seems that we have both gone through a process of torture just to be dead. I am hoping that talking can bring us together.

Tell me, are we the only ones to know, the only ones who understand?

Not sure, but part of me wants to be with you.

Will talking make you touch me?

I don't want to touch you anywhere private just yet. It is difficult to explain.

What do you want to talk about?

Shame.

What about it?

It hurts. It hurts badly.

What makes you feel ashamed?

I am ugly and you are beautiful.

No, you are not.

...

I remember the shame. Shame is ... is laughter ... laughter, always. Not once, not occasionally, but always. I remember it in every moment whilst my eyes were awake – laughter ... because of who I was, of the way I am. Shamed constantly, a bombardment of abuse, a hammering away at me, pounding me down, subjugating me into avoidance. As I am me, I am to be laughed at.

And now, do you hear the laughter?

I still hear it today, yes. It echoes through time, it is what makes me look down. Raise my head, and I am exposed to the humiliation.

I will not humiliate you.

Laughter when I am awake. Laughter when I am asleep.

Such cruelty.

Laughter when I smile. Laughter when I don't smile.

How could anyone –

Everyone could and everyone did. What right did I have to smile? How dare I do that!

I like your smile, it is beautiful.

How dare I inflict this unnaturalness on the world?!

Your smile makes my heart beat faster. Can you hear it?

It has wanted to make my heart sleep in silence.

No!

Sometimes … sometimes … I wished it could be so.

I am fortunate that it is not so.

Do you know what it means to be lonely? To hide away just so that you never have to experience the battering noise of laughter? Can you hear the laughter? Can you hear it?

I hear no laughter, but I see it. I see it in your stooping head. I see it in the long hair that you grow so that you can hide your face. I can see it in your reticence.

Yes, it all conceals my shame.

I see the fear in your body. I see your emotional hunger. I feel it as your body is pressed up against mine.

Is my body funny?

It is beautiful!

Do I look funny?

No.

Can you see the self-loathing?

Your face is beautiful.

How can you say that? ... People understand, when you are not normal on one side of your face – your cheeks, your ears, something that effects only one half – they think something has happened. When you have something wrong with the central part of your face – your nose, your lips, perhaps your eyes – if you are deformed or disfigured, then people see you as a freak ... It is to do with your identity. People do not want to identify with it when your deformity is to that central part of your face, it seems you have no humanity: miss an arm or a leg and people understand; miss a nose or a lip then you are something not to be touched, someone not to talk to or someone not to be near.

I have similar difficulties with my body.

I am not competing with you and your experiences – but you can walk down a street with clothes covering your body and you look relatively normal. I cannot walk around with a paper bag over my head.

Yes, that is true ... Are you crying?

Trying to hold it in.

Oh, darling –

No, no, don't move. Stay where you are. Stay with your back to me.

But –

No! Please.

Okay.

You do not know how much the shame hurts.

I do ... although my shame is different. Yours is a face shame. Mine is a body shame.

If I tell you about my shame then you will understand why I don't want to look into your eyes right now.

It does that to you, doesn't it?

People crush you and some don't even know it: the power of their eyes makes you lower yours.

Yes, life crushes you. Life shames us.

What is your shame?

I have had bad thoughts. About wanting to hurt people. Sometimes I want to hurt myself. I am not sure if it is me or other people that are causing my problems. I just don't know.

The operations were not the worst thing: it is what happens before and after.

I remember when I was younger, a little girl, perhaps ten or eleven. I remember waking up and finding it painful to move, and also when I was playing, I could feel that things were different. I told my mother and she took me to the doctor.

I was at an age where I had started to develop – I had little girl's breasts. As a girl I was so aware of my body and the changes that were happening. I was self-conscious about the changes and couldn't wait to be fully grown.

The doctor needed to examine me. He asked me to undress down to my underwear. He looked at my back and told me to take my mini-bra off. It was the first time I had felt embarrassed. I saw him staring at my chest. He asked me if he could look under my arms and I let him. Then he put his finger inside my knickers and pulled the top of them away from my body, so that he could have a peep at my sex. Mother did not say anything.

He asked me to turn around and clasp my hands together. He asked me to keep my knees and feet together and bend forward so that my hands would dangle towards the floor. I could not understand why any boy – or man – would want to look at my backside. I felt humiliated and I did not understand.

It was the first time that I felt that other people could make me feel a certain way about my body. It felt so intrusive.

After the X-ray was brought in, the doctor had a discussion with myself and Mother. He told me that I had the beginnings of scoliosis and that my spine would curve as I grow. I did not know what that meant until he showed me the X-ray.

I had a double curve: one in the upper back and another in the lower, curving in opposite directions. That S shape, that river that you see on my back, is the shape of my spine.

He said that the curvature of my spine had caused asymmetries in my body; that he had seen that one breast was going to develop slightly lower than the other; that my neckline, waistline, shoulder-line and chest wall were all asymmetrical. He said that when he asked me to bend over he could see a rib hump forming on the right side of my back and the shape of the spine could be seen.

I wanted to cry at that moment but I could see that my mother was shocked.

The doctor said that the size of my breasts and the amount of under-arm and pubic hair indicated the level of physical maturity I was at, and that I had a long way to grow through puberty. The curves of my spine and distortions of my body would have that same opportunity to grow, making my body worse.

Not only did I feel the horror of what he said, but for the first time I felt the horror of people's eyes all over my body: he had found out something about me that I would not want any boy to know.

I was told that to prevent my condition getting worse I need to wear a brace – that it had to be tight so that the pressure on the curve on my spine would begin to correct it, or at least not make it worse.

I knew that I had to wear one, because my clothes were not fitting properly, walking long distances was becoming a problem, and when my parents tried to hug me, I could feel the awkwardness of my body and the boniness of it in areas where it should not be bony. When I looked in the mirror, in my mind I was trying to fight what my body might become; and my body was fighting the images in my mind, of my dreams, my future – one without scoliosis. My body was changing into something that it did not want to be and that I had no control over. I thought, perhaps, the brace would be a way of gaining control over my body.

Because of my double curve, the rotation of my spine, the asymmetry of my body and other issues, I started wearing the brace. It was specially designed for me – a combination of braces, moulded for the contours of my body.

When I saw the type of brace that they wanted me to wear, I was in shock; my stomach started to turn and my heart sank. Not only was I considered deformed, but I would have to wear a brace that looked like a medieval contraption, which would make everyone aware of my body – public humiliation. What boy would ever want me? I would be enclosed in a plastic shell compressing me from my waist, from just over my hips, to right under my arms, and metal bars projecting upwards and out from the shell, that stretched my neck, elongating my spine. There was one bar in front, supporting my chin, and two bars at the back of my head, at the base of the skull, all these metal bars connected at the top by a circular metal ring around my neck.

I could hear in my head, in my mind, people's voices talking about me. I could feel their eyes all over my body and the look on their faces imprinted in my eyes. Every doctor and nurse was being positive to me, and all I was feeling was something diametrically opposite.

I had to strip naked. I was made to wear two body stockings. The first was see-through and I was aware that people could see my naked body – it did not feel nice. Even after the second went on you could see the lie of the land. Then I had to hold on to some straps which hung from the ceiling, and my head was placed in a halter – one strap under my chin and another supporting the back of my head at the base of my skull. They then lifted me slightly, to stretch my spine, and it felt like my feet would barely remain on the floor.

They placed gauze around my body, over my body stockings, from the top of my chest down to just below my hips. After that, they spread plaster all over the gauze, feeling my landscape as they did so. It did not feel as if my body still had the right to its own integrity.

I had to wait a short time until the plaster hardened. As it dried, I could feel the mould tightening. It felt like I was suffocating slowly, the life being squeezed out of me. First there was the hanging, and now the suffocation. My body only felt free again once the mould was dried and cut open.

Two weeks later, I went to collect my brace, and when I saw it, it felt like a death sentence. It was real and it was for me to wear now. It was so constricting that it did not allow much upper body movement. The pad for my left hip was pushing it down. There were other pads where the bends of my spine were, pushing inward. My breasts were trapped under the tight brace. It wrapped under my arms. A metal chin-rest supported me at the front and a neck-rest supported me at the back, keeping my spine straighter, but restricting my movement so that I could hardly even look down. My body breathed through little holes in the plastic brace. They were there to make my torture last longer – for my body to survive and yet not to survive.

All I heard at the time was that I had to wear the brace for sixteen hours a day. It seemed endless. I went home and cried.

One time, I looked at my body without my brace, when I felt it wasn't helping much. My body was destroying the image of the perfect woman I wanted to be. That image subsequently disintegrated, leaving me with my new realities: a man who wanted me for me, who undressed me, who touched me, who made love to me – and then left me because he could not accept the body I had; another, who went out with me because he thought I should be grateful; another, who just laughed at me when he saw my body. But the one that hurt the most was the first – a boy at school, where I thought everyone had accepted me. We made love and the next day at school he started teasing me in front of others. They all joined in. And I found out why. He had posted a naked picture of me, taken when I was asleep, all over the school. My body was no longer mine, and I felt ashamed.

The teasing outside destroyed me inside. That was why I went out with other boys: I was trying to convince myself that my body was more valuable than what that first boy thought and that he was the only idiot out there. But eventually other people and the world itself infiltrate you, not only with their stares but with the expectation of humiliation and shame. I could no longer separate that from myself, just like the brace which had become a part of me, embedding itself in me. My enclosed body was safer hiding behind the brace. Though I knew I had lost the battle both with my body and with myself.

I don't think you will humiliate me. In fact I know you won't. But this shame is embedded in me. My body is no longer separate from it. I cannot have true freedom. That's why I want you to tear me apart, to deconstruct me, to take this brace away.

No, I can't. I won't hurt you.

You won't hurt me.

I am not going to do anything that will hurt you.

For me to be free, it has to be done. Otherwise, the struggle has ended in defeat.

Your physical battle was lost as a teenager or young woman. My battle was lost by being born. I never had the opportunity to be "normal" and then have to fight to regain it, or even to see something that was escaping me. I believe it is worse if you have something like this from birth than to acquire it later in life. I do not mean to belittle you, your troubles or your feelings in any way, or say they are not worthy – it is just that I know no other way.

I know; I know you do not mean any harm.

Just like you, mine was a battle between myself and others. "Myself" was never "whole", I was what other people saw – nothing inside was saying "I do not want to be that way". My only dream was to be invisible to others so that I could avoid the horrors of what people saw. I only knew that I was what other people saw. And now, when I catch people's eyes, I no longer capture their horror. I believe that my eyes project the horror and offence: it is me who causes others to be uncomfortable.

The shame I experienced was unrelenting. Even before I knew what shame was, a sadness dawned on me.

If you remain quiet for a bit you can hear the laughter and the teasing … Can you hear it?

No.

I can. Even when I am alone.

The relentless pounding of what you hear soon becomes the truth. How can it be possible for everyone to behave in the same way? … As they say, truth hurts.

I was once told that when I was born, when my mother saw me, she wanted to push me back in. Can you imagine what that does to a child who already believes he is the horror that other people see? An immediate rejection, by the one who gave birth to you? But at the heart of that is that you feel there is an element of truth in it because you have already been rejected by all – why would my mother then not reject me? Am I so unworthy of living that the very birth of the child was a horror in itself?

It is when you hear such things from others that you know it is about the complete and utter rejection of you as a person. It is not that the space between myself and others increases infinitely, it is that I am not worthy of that space.

Even just in growing up, in just being me, I felt ashamed. What was it people saw about my face that made them drop their smiles when they noticed that you were looking at them? Every smile I saw dropped, after they caught me looking at them; I felt like I had ruined their day – completely slammed! That this body, this space, this human being, a child, could ruin someone's day just by being themselves.

You begin to notice that people avoid sitting next to you, wherever you are, as if what you have is contagious. Not once, not twice, but time and again. Rejection.

Parents with young children, not letting them near you, taking them away. Or children happily playing and wanting to approach you, then suddenly stopping and turning away after having had a closer look at you, then going back to their parents to whisper something about you as they point in your direction. Rejection.

Others looking at you and laughing. Rejection.

People not wanting to shake your hands or give you a hug, even though you are only a child – which manifested later into my uncertainty about whether to hug someone, or simply not hugging someone so as to avoid a negative reaction. People not wanting to sit next to you on a train or in a waiting room. Going into shops where they would rather place the change on the counter than in your hands, when you have just seen them place it in the previous customer's hand. Their reticence ingrained in you forever when you meet others. Rejection again.

Then there are those trying to be kind, who speak to you slowly and/or loudly, making assumptions about your intellect purely based on appearance.

And when you feel good and happy, and you happen to smile, for them to then burst into laughter because of your imperfect smile. They would not ever mirror my smile; it was just laughter. A disfigured person smiling was another, additional form of disfigurement to the non-disfigured face looking at you. Rejection.

When I heard someone say that my face looked like a half-chewed-up toffee, my breath stopped, the world became distant, and I isolated. Was that what people saw? Do you know what a half-chewed-up toffee looks like? Even I hated that image; no wonder people treated me the way they did. It was difficult to take, as a child – everybody's behaviour confirmed my appearance. Rejection.

It's like being assaulted from all different directions. The teasing becomes something physical being hurled at you – stones or garbage being thrown at you constantly. A bombardment of messages to say that you do not belong amongst them; that you are not part of their humanity. And each tease has an exponential impact compared to the previous one, because you could not handle the previous one. I simply could not brave it any longer.

When you have heard, throughout your childhood, other children laughing, it penetrates you. Every whisper you may hear, every time you see someone talking, you become unable to decide whether they are talking about you or not. Rejection.

And it wasn't just about all these external images infiltrating my mind; it was the fact of the avoidance of touch. Imagine a child growing up and not being held, not being touched – crying, wanting comfort, but everybody moving away. How does that child grow up? What does that child become? Lost? Detached from the world? Do they occupy a space in a world of others where you are not "being-with" those others? Rejection.

It is about people stopping you as you walk down the street, just so they can have a good look, and then laughing when they know you are feeling humiliated. What right do they have to strip you of your dignity?

I don't like looking at people any more: I don't want to be battered by their gaze or laughter. It's best to grow my hair long and to stoop my head to ensure my face is hidden.

Being ashamed is feeling a stigma when people stare at you. Being ashamed is feeling that you do not have the right to be happy. Being ashamed is feeling more comfortable being rejected than when engaging with others. Being ashamed is not wanting to go out, just to avoid it all – wanting to be safe on your own. Being ashamed is hearing other people's laughter in your mind as you sleep. Being ashamed is not liking yourself.

– *Lies!*

Lies?!

DISTORTION

They are all lies!

I am not lying to you.

From what you have been saying, the smiles of others are like weapons – the truth only seems to come when they withdraw their smiles. They think one thing and do another. Even when these smiles are captured in photographs, the photos lie. People look happy in these photos but you cannot see what lies behind their eyes – their story, their life. Captured for a split second is a momentary joy – or, more likely, a false joy – a smile. I avoid these kinds of photo, they just remind me of the hurt and pain that I see in myself, or the hidden secrets that they do not want anyone to share – the history of their actions, of their guilt.

Mirrors tell the truth. They show all your perfections and imperfections as they are – no hiding. I could never look in the mirror if anyone else was near – I did not want to know that other people saw my truth. My horror is fine on its own, but the stigma becomes too much if someone else is there to see it.

Yes, I feel the stigma. Their eyes creep all over you while the burning sensation of their gaze hits your body.

Yes, that's how it is – that burning sensation.

The destruction and devastation of your past is plain to see. They live with the lie, we live with the truth.

They want it that way. They burn us for who we are.

They don't know what they leave behind. They don't care.

What can we do?

I want you to do something for me. I want you to turn around.

Not yet.

I find it too uncomfortable, with my body, to be on the floor for so long. I am going to sit up. I want you to turn around and look at me.

You want that burning sensation?

No, I don't get that with you. I want you to turn around and I want you not to be scared.

I am not scared of you. I would not be here half naked if I was.

I need you to turn around. Promise you won't be scared; promise me you won't run away.

What?

No! Don't turn around just yet. Promise me first.

What's going on?

Promise me, please.

I promise I won't run away.

Close your eyes. Sit up and turn around.

...

Now what?

Promise?

I promise.

Open your eyes.

Oh my god! What's happened? What's happened to you?

You promised you would not run away.

No, no, I am not running away. It's ... it's just a bit of a shock. What's happened to you?

Talking about it all makes it happen. Remembering and reliving it makes it happen: hearing your story, empathising, relating it to my own seems to stimulate all those emotions inside. Even though you may think I am the stronger one, I am finding it so difficult being with you, as I need acceptance myself.

But what are they? Blotches? Hives?

Eyes!

Eyes?

Look carefully and you will see that they look like eyes, that they <u>are</u> eyes. Come and look closer. You can see them … they are real eyes.

Oh my god! They are so real! … Look! I can see the whites and the curvature of the eyeballs … and the irises are also different colours.

They are real. Different people, different eyes. This is what happens to me when I feel the pain of others looking at me. Their stares are imprinted on my body. I am no longer myself but the horror in their eyes.

I know about their stares.

It burns every time they gaze at certain parts of my body. They do not see me for who I am.

I wanted to pull away at first, not because I do not like you, but because it was unexpected.

I know. Your eyes do not burn me. You have seen me before and I know your eyes are gentle. Your reaction to me was of genuine surprise but not horror. I would be scared as well if this suddenly happened to you. I call it a disease: the judgement of others. When you used the word "stigma", I felt all the experiences and sensations of the past come up. It stings and prints my body wherever they stared. When they look at my spine their eyes are imprinted there. When they look at the unevenness of my breasts, their eyes are imprinted there. It is the same with my ribs, my hips and the little hump on my back. Whether I have clothes on or not, I can feel their eyes burn my body. Yet the people looking at me see nothing.

How am I able to see them?

I want you too much. These are the memories of the past and talking through them has revived them.

I am sorry.

No, don't be. It has taught me something – I can have a shared private space without judgement …

Take them off me for me, please.

How?

Peel them off.

Are you sure?

Yes, I want you to.

Will it destroy the memories?

No. It will only take away what I am feeling now.

Where shall I start?

With my spine.

You had best turn around, then.

Here you are, I am ready.

Are you sure?

Yes.

I am just going to lift the corner of one of them.

…

Ouch! –

Sorry!

No, carry on; otherwise, you'll be saying sorry all the time. It will be painful for me, but carry on. It feels like a very strong sticking plaster being pulled off, ripping my skin along with it.

They're so real. I don't want to touch them.

If you want to be with me then you must.

Okay.

…

I have just lifted the corner of one of them but it looks like they have gone in deep, so I'll have to dig into your skin to lift them out.

Pull, just pull them out!

It may scar you.

My skin will heal.

Here goes, then …

Owww!

It has left a bit of a crater behind.

Do the next one.

Are you sure?

Yes. Don't worry about me.

One, two, three …

Oowww! That hurt!

I have just noticed that the redness of the first one has already gone.

It's healing. Carry on, do them all.

Even the ones on your breasts?

Everywhere! I don't want their eyes to hurt me any more.

Let me finish here first.

…

It's all done. The skin is healing, the redness is fading, and the craters have almost gone from most of them.

The rest will follow and my skin will be normal again. It is only the expressions of my emotions and memories that you have removed from the surface of my skin. They are still inside me but you have stopped them from burning me.

I don't understand. Why does something like this not happened to me?

It does. You just can't see it.

See what?

Your mask.

I don't have a mask on. I am what you see.

Just as I have body shame, you have your face shame. Just as my brace has surrounded me, melded itself with me and I am unable to take it off, so your mask surrounds your face. You are a man in a mask. Something you cannot separate yourself from.

I don't feel anything.

It's all psychological. It's all symbolic. We are held back by the burdens of what society has done to us: these are our manacles and shackles, our punishment for violating their norms.

Yes, like criminals, we have to be locked down.

Imprisoned in our body brace or face mask.

Punished!

Don't you know all criminals are ugly?

They are all monsters!

And all the victims are beautiful and innocent ... like angels. We are the perpetrators of their horror.

And others think that we have somehow deserved all this. That we are this way because we have done something bad. That in a previous life we were bad.

They condemn us from the outside. They condemn us from the inside.

Either way, we are condemned to a mediaeval mask or an unopenable brace.

It might as well be a chastity belt to prevent us from being together.

Yes, monsters and criminals must not be allowed to procreate.

That's one of their hidden thoughts – justifiable eugenics.

We can't let that happen: allow people to control our lives through their own ignorance.

Rip me, rip me apart, slice me open.

No!

You must. We must get rid of it all. I need you to see me without all the layers, see me without the shame, see me naked.

I can't. I won't.

You must journey with me. We are so near one another.

I'm not going to hurt you.

No, you won't. I do not mean literally. We must imagine it. We must believe it to be true. Only when we are convinced of that can we be free together.

I don't know.

This is not a game. We don't have an endless amount of time. I thought you wanted to be with me. I thought you wanted to experience being with someone. If we can't move forward then what is there? It is something we have to do. Years of pain and torture have enmeshed the brace into me – others have forced it upon us. In your case, you cannot move forward with all those masks on – these things prevent us from being ourselves. They are constantly being put on us by others, to imprison us within our own skins. But I can see you don't want to … that you can't even be with me.

No, it's not true.

We can't overcome what we have to overcome unless we remove these chains, these fetters and entrapments.

I know, but I do not want to hurt you.

You're not going to hurt me! It's all in here, in our minds, in our imaginations. But it has to be real; we have to believe it is happening. Only then can we shed their gazes, their torture, their humiliation.

Their laughter.

Their laughter – gone. Only then can we be free.

You know, deep inside, that it is true and that if you and I want to be together then we need to be free of all of this. How much more painful can it be? We have gone through so much. You have already seen me almost completely naked. We are nearly together in any case.

What are we to do?

Trust in me and let me guide you. If you start on me then you can see the impact it can have.

What do you want me to do?

Slice me open, tear me apart.

But –

Listen. It's all here, in the mind. Not out there. You must be able to visualise it, to feel it, to enact it. You have to commit to it and the moment you have any doubt will be the moment that shame will re-infect you. It has to be real – no believing then disbelieving; no differentiation between reality and imagination – it has to be real. Just think, in a short while we may be free from the burdens of the world. What price would you pay to share that with someone you want to be with?

I want to be with you.

I believe you. I believe <u>in</u> you. Do you <u>believe</u> we are a few steps away from being together?

Yes.

Do you want to take these steps?

I do, especially now, when I am here with you.

Do you believe that these steps will be a journey with me? A journey for us to take?

Yes.

Don't worry, then. We'll take it hand in hand. I am not going to tease you.

I believe.

…

I want you to hoist me up.

Up where?

Look above you.

I can't see anything.

You need to believe it to be real. I need you to believe it's real. Look above you – can you see it?

Yes, yes, I can.

Take the rope. Pull it down and tie my hands together.

I need to get up.

Don't worry I will close my eyes.

…

I've got the rope.

Tie it around my wrists ... Tighter. It needs to support my weight.

How's this?

Yes, perfect. Now, pull back the sheet from over my feet and you will see another rope anchored to the floor.

I see it.

Tie that rope around my ankles, so that I am also anchored to the floor.

Done.

Now go to the other end of the rope that you tied my hands with, and pull it. The pulley should hoist me up and my feet should remain attach to the rope that's connected to the floor.

...

I have the rope now.

Pull!

I am pulling.

Pull!

Your sheet has fallen off.

Just pull!

Are you okay?

Yes. Pull! ... Pull!

Am I hurting you?

Pull! Pull!

I'm nearly there.

Yes, stretch me ... Stretch me a bit more.

It's getting more difficult.

Argh!

Should I stop?

Stretch me as much as you can.

I can't stretch any more.

Tie the end of the rope to the hook on the floor over there so that you do not have to keep hold of it.

It's tied.

What do you see when you look at me?

I see you struggling for breath.

What else do you see? Remember: the truth.

I see you hanging by your arms. Your body being stretched. Your feet lifted yet anchored by a rope to the floor.

What else do you see?

I see your body from behind. You're completely naked. I see your rib hump. I see your shoulder blade sticking out.

What about my spine?

I see your scar; I see the river.

Does it meander?

It meanders slightly. It meanders less than before.

Yes, you are making me look normal. Come around to the front ... What do you see?

I see your beautiful landscape.

Do you see the peaks and troughs?

I see them. They have lessened. Just like the angle of your hip-line. Just like the angle of your neckline.

Can you see my sex?

I can see your triangle.

Finger me!

No! What good would that do?

I want to experience pleasure when I am not so distorted.

No, not while you are hooked up and are barely able to breathe.

Take that scalpel. The one over there.

Where?

Over to your left, on the floor.

I see it. What do you want me to do with it?

Pick it up.

What now?

Come near me ... come close up ... look at my body. Look carefully. What do you see? Can you see the brace that envelops it? Can you?

I can see it. I can see it tightly wrapped around your torso. It looks very tight.

That's why I can't breathe properly. It's been constraining all these years. Can you see the material it is made from?

Yes, yes, I can see that it is made from the judgement of others.

Yes, now you believe!

I can see your body desperate to be released. I can see the poverty of and the hunger for freedom.

Roll your finger along my neckline.

Like this?

Harder ... Scratch me. Let me see the marks ...

There is hardly any blood drawn. There are no tears on my skin; do it again. This time harder.

My nails cannot cut you.

Use the scalpel. Cut away these judgements from my flesh.

Are you sure?

It's like the eyes. The ones that were all over my body. Only you can see it. Only those who care can see it … Cut me free, please!

Okay, I'm going to press as hard as I can – I don't want you to suffer any more.

Yes, do that.

Here I go.

That's it … Right to left … oh … Oh. Argh! Argh!

Cutting you is magical. The scalpel – it leaves a trail of blood. It's freeing you. The blood is cascading down your torso.

There! What now?

Do the same for my hip-line. Cut me from one hip to the other.

When I cut you, the lip of your open wound seems so raw, it goes so red, bleeding within moments, seeking its freedom.

Ow!

You're flinching!

You're cutting me. It's painful ... ow ... Ow ... OW ...

I know. It looks painful. But if you flinch it's not going to be straight.

I don't care, just cut me.

I'm not happy.

Just do it! Don't stop halfway!

... It's done!

Now cut me from the middle of my neckline to the middle of my hip-line. I want you to open me up straight down the middle. I want all the poison of others to drain from me.

Are you sure?

Yes.

I should wait.

No.

You need to catch your breath.

No, just do it, it will be easier.

I'm going to do it quickly, then.

Just do it! Let me get rid of the bad blood that's inside me.

I'm slicing you open, tearing your skin apart.

I can feel it. I can feel the release. It's good to be alive.

The blood just keeps pouring out.

It will stop: it's what happens when the hurt penetrates your blood. The hatred, the humiliation, the pain needs to come out.

It's disgusting. What do you want me to do now?

Put your hands inside the vertical cut and peel back the skin – like two flaps.

I am peeling it … It's hard to pull them open. It's hard to separate your skin from your muscles and bone.

Pull, pull as hard as you can.

Can you hear to tearing noise? It sounds like –

Argh! Argh!

Your muscles and bones do not want to let go.

Just imagine it is part of my brace – tear it back, rip it apart.

I am tearing! … Ripping!

Argh! Argh!

The two flaps of your skin are hanging open now.

Just wait a few minutes … I need to get my breath back … It's painful.

I'm sorry. I'm sorry that I have done this to you.

I needed to get rid of the pain and only you could have done it.

Have I become a monster?

No. If you were a monster, I would be dead by now.

Are you sure you want to go on?

Yes, in a few moments or so.

…

I want you to put your hands inside me now, between the two sets of ribs and pull them apart, rip them away from my body.

You're making me feel sick.

I need you to do it.

Why?

The brace embedded itself in me. My ribs are the brace. I don't want it to be a part of me any more. No more mediaeval contraption for me … Please … Just think of it like the eyes that you peeled off – my body will heal itself. You will not have hurt me.

…

I'm going to put my hands in now, and I'm going to pull out your ribs.

Rip them out!

I will rip them out, but only if you promise me something.

Anything, just do it; anything. Just free me from this.

As I rip them out I want you to tell all those people who have hurt you, all those people who stared at you, I want you to tell them what you feel about them. I want you to believe that when I rip your ribs out, the hurt and pain will go with it. Promise me you will?

I promise.

Are you ready?

Yes.

I'm just placing my hands between the two sets of ribs.

Yes, go on, that's it!

No. No, I can't do it.

You must. You cannot leave me this way.

Is there no other way?

Don't deny me this. Don't deny me my freedom. Don't think about it, just do it.

Close your eyes, then. I can't do it if you look at me.

Eyes closed ... Well? ... Argh! That hurts!

Should I stop?

No ... Keep going.

Well?

"Well" what?

Your promise?

Okay. Okay. Just go in further ... Argh! ... Get lost, girls at school.

"Get lost"! Is that all you have? Is that all you want to say to them?!
I am inside your body trying to rip out your ribs and all you can
say is "Get lost"?

Argh! ... Fuck off you bitches!

That's it!

Fuck off for teasing me! Fuck off for making my life so difficult!

More!

Fuck off doctors for diagnosing me! Fuck off for telling me my life will change forever!

Go on!

Fuck off the doctors who operated on me! Fuck off for giving me these scars! Fuck off for the infection and the failed operations, Fuck off! Fuck off for not making it work!

Trying to get in between your bones and muscles. Go on.

Argh! Fuck off people who are talking about me!

More –

Fuck off to all those eyes looking at me ... argh!! ... I hope you all fucking die!

My hands are in place around your ribs.

Fuck off you boys who humiliated me ... fuck off ... argh!! ... Fuck off boys who slept with me!

Pulling now.

Fuck off to the world for being so cruel to me!

I'm going to pull your ribcage apart now.

Fuck off, Mother ... argh! Argh! ...

It's bending ...

Fuck off, Mother, for giving this to me ...

Cracking now.

Fuck off, Mother!.

And ripping them out.

FUCK OFF!!

...

Did you hear it crack?

I heard nothing.

You did not hear your ribs break?

I was too busy screaming at the world!

Here. Let me hold you. Let me hug you.

…

Fuck off, Mother! … Fuck off!

…

You whispered something about your mother in my ear. Do you hate your mother?

I hate her for giving me this. I just did not want all of this. Why, Mum, why? Why did I have to have this?

…

It's okay. I'm all right now. Just wasn't expecting it.

I'm going to set you down now.

Wait.

Hey!

Those ribs you ripped out of my body – throw them away. I don't want them anywhere near me.

Where do you want me to throw them?

Just discard them over there.

...

Watch me throw them. I am going to do your right side first, the one that is giving you a bit of a hump ... Ready? ... Here you go.

It's strange seeing it fly away in the air, rotating – convex and concave, convex then concave.

What do you mean?

It's like a landscape and all its different formations – it veers from being one thing to being another.

Do you mean your body landscape?

Yes. And the peaks and troughs of my emotions – removed.

You can say goodbye to those emotions again: watch me throw your left ribs now.

Fuck off emotions! Fuck off cruel world!

...

I want to come down now.

Yes, I'll bring you down now. Let me go behind you to get the rope … I've got it. Am going to lower you now. Your body is heavy on this rope.

Don't drop me!

It's okay. Your feet are about to touch the floor so don't be frightened … you're nearly back on the floor now …

Lower me to my knees.

Are you on your knees safely?

Yes, but I am falling sideways.

Holding tighter … gently now: your head is nearing the floor … Okay?

Come and look at me, see what you have done.

Your body is not open any more; just the cut marks where I opened you up and the blood around them.

Keep watching.

The blood around those marks is also disappearing.

I can breathe better now.

The blood is gone. Just the red rawness and the scars are left.

I am a bit tired.

And even that is healing up. The scars are disappearing!

See, I told you you wouldn't hurt me.

There is no trace of what I have done to you. Not a mark on you!

It's real, but it's not real.

Even the blood, which was everywhere, has all gone. What happened?

I'm okay now ... Come and hold me ... Give me a big squeeze ... No, keep my hands tight and don't unravel the rope at my feet. I want them to remain tied, also.

Why?

I want you to do one more thing. I want you to straighten my spine.

Wasn't the stretching good enough for you?

No. That teenage girl in me wants her idealised image, and I want you to give it to her.

You want to be perfect?

I want to be perfectly free from all those emotions.

What do you want me to do, then?

Turn me over, so that I am lying on my front.

Hold on a second ... Let me get around to your side to turn you over ... There!

Keep my body stretched.

I'll take the rest of the rope and pull it out of the hoist and hook it up to the pulley on the floor over there. I'll stretch you like I did before, but this time along the floor.

Yes, pull me one way and then another. Stretch me.

Hold on ... I'm pulling!

Yes, Pull! ... Pull!

How's this?

Not so tight this time.

Okay ... How about now?

That's fine. Now pick up that machete, over there to your left.

What?

Pick up that machete.

Are you sure?

Don't doubt me. Believe in me.

It's heavy.

Stand behind and astride me.

Now what?

Pierce my skin with the blade of the machete. Pierce it along the length of my scar. Divide that river that runs from top to bottom. Open me up like the doctors did.

Are you sure?

Believe me.

I believe.

Then do it!

Okay! ... I'm cutting ...

Expose my spine, set it free ... Ow! the pain!

Are you okay?

I am alive! ...

I am slicing you open and your skin is so eager to expose you, it retreats from the cut as I slice it – as if it knows you want it to.

It does, it does!

Am I hurting you?

Cut; cut all the way down.

The blood is filling up the cavern in the open wound, spilling over and the line of the cut.

Don't you just love the horror of it all?!

I don't want to be the cause of your horror.

You are not. The machete is my saviour and you are too.

It sounds so romantic.

It is. And I want to dance with you.

How shall we dance?

I want you to hack out my spine! Hack it out. Don't be polite. Its rudeness needs to be met with some brutality.

I need to pull your skin wider apart first.

I can feel the air along my spine ... It's finally breathing.

How do you want me to take it out?

Hack on either side of it.

Ready? ... Here I go!

Argh!

Hacking again.

Argh!

Again.

Argh ... Harder! Harder!

I'm hacking.

That's it! Wow, it's amazing! Harder!

I am.

Argh! ... And on the other side of the spine.

Yes.

Argh! Argh!

I'm hacking, I'm hacking, I'm hacking!

Do it again and again and again!

It's beautiful! It's beautiful!

Did you hear the sound it made?

Sound of freedom?

Of possibilities!

It's done.

Thank you.

Did you see all the blood come out? Look how widely it has splattered.

Like a painting on a blank canvas.

I am an artist!

Take my spine out.

Yes, let me lift your spine out now ... Putting my hands in ... Just digging out all the muscle and scraping away all the tendons... I've – I've – I've got hold of it now.

Yank it out ... Argh! Argh! Wait! Wait! I think it's still connected to my skull and my pelvis.

Hold on. Let me hack the two ends off.

Yes, yes, no mercy!

Ready? One, two ... three!

Ow! Argh! Argh!

Nearly done.

Argh! Argh!

There, that's your neck done. Now for your pelvic girdle.

Take it out! Take it out!

One. Two. Three.

Argh!

Hold on a minute. Let me get my hands around the spine again.

Pull! Pull!

Pulling ...

Argh! Pull! Pull!

It's coming!

Argh! … Harder! Faster! … Argh!

I am trying.

Yank it!

I am!

Again!

I've done it, I've done it!

Yes! YES!! … Finally, I feel free!

What should I do with your spine?

Shake it! Whip it! Whip it into shape! Iron out the bends!

Hold on. Let me get into position … Okay … I'm whipping it!

Again … Again … Do it until it's straight.

Can you hear the cracking of the whips?

I hear them. It's lovely hearing my spine being cracked into shape!

Your blood is everywhere.

Get rid of all that infection – my hatred of other people – which has surrounded my spine.

It's amazing!

Whip it!

I am.

Whip it harder!

It's done, it's done … Look, I think it's done now.

Show me.

See.

I can't raise my head. Come this way.

See.

Yes, I can see it. It's beautiful. <u>You're</u> beautiful.

When I put this back inside you, you will be beautiful too.

Being straight is beautiful?

No. Being free is beautiful.

Yes, slot it in.

I'm just plugging it back into your neck ...

Ow!! ... I can move my head a bit more now.

And the other end into your pelvic girdle – just pressing down on the pelvis so that it can slot in easily.

I can feel it clicking into place.

Hold on ... There you go.

Yes, I think I can move my legs now.

That's good!

I want you to zip me back up again, zip me up and put my skin back together with a straight spine in my body.

When I zip you up, the source of the trail of blood along your spine begins to disappear as I go … And now, as I move up to the top of your spine, the blood seems to be catching up, and so does the disappearance. The zip has left traces of its teeth along your spine. They are like stitches all the way from your pelvis to your neck … They are beautiful.

Are you not scared of them?

No. My body is littered with them. They are you and I am here.

I know, and I am so grateful.

If it's okay I am going to untie your hands.

…

I feel better now.

While I was looking at you, I did not notice that the blood all around had disappeared. The rawness of the stitches and the soreness of your skin around your zip scar has also gone. I think your back has healed. I can see the S shape again and your old scar has returned.

I'm just going to turn around.

Are you okay?

Yes. Do you like my body now?

I have always liked it.

Does it seem any different to you now?

It seems the same. But I see the difference in you.

You have not even noticed.

What have I not noticed?

That I'm lying here completely naked in front of you.

I think I forgot about that.

Can you untie my feet?

Sure.

You are so gentle with your hands.

I don't want to hurt you.

Thank you … Stay there for a second.

You want me to do more things?

114

I just opened my legs for you. What do you see?

I see your vagina.

Do you not want to touch it? ... Well?

Vaginas – they are like chewed-up toffees. Why when the world is rejecting a chewed-up face like mine would I want to touch something that constitutes a rejection?

Because your face is nothing like a chewed-up toffee. Faces are not to be feared. It is the imagery in your head that needs to be faced.

That imagery is not separate from my face any more – it *is* my face. What happens if I confront my fears and I still hate my face and still dislike vaginas? Then it may be impossible to be with someone.

You don't have to face them on your own. It's <u>our</u> journey. Together. You helped me and I want to help you. In everything you have said there has been a difference in who you believe you are and what others see you as. You just have to let go of the images that others perceive and you are left with only one side of the equation – your belief in yourself.

When I see your vagina, I see the horrors that other people see in me – I see that toffee. Who wants a fucked-up chewed up mess?

Let me help you let it go.

They used to call me "Fuck-face" – a fucked-up face. I don't want to be a fuck-face any more.

I know, darling. I know.

…

Lie down next to me.

Back to back?

No, beside me, on our backs.

Did I hurt you?

No.

It felt like I did.

It had to be real.

How can it be real and an illusion at the same time?

Reality is an illusion. Nobody knows what it is aside from their own experience.

Is my experience the truth?

It's real.

So, what is the illusion?

We have both created an illusion to block out reality. We did it so much that it became automatic. That's when illusion and reality are difficult to distinguish, get blurred, become distorted.

I am a monster to others.

But, deep down, you know this is an illusion.

You are right. I do not know the difference.

You know what I would like to do to you?

No.

I would like to rip your face off.

That would be wonderful.

It would, wouldn't it?

To throw away my face.

To start afresh.

I would not have to trawl through illusion or reality to deal with the distortion.

What would it mean to you?

I am not sure. I have been with it all my life. Whatever it is, it is a part of me.

And has that made you happy?

The world has made me unhappy.

It's still making you unhappy.

My own private unhappiness, that's what it is.

But that's not all. It affects me as well.

You're beautiful.

Are we on a journey?

Yes.

Will you believe?

Yes.

Are you ready to believe one hundred per cent? No distinction between reality and imagination?

Yes.

Come on! Get up.

Hey?

No – actually, stay there. I am just going to sit on top of you. Sit astride you.

What are you going to do?

Give me your arms. No! – put them down by your sides, under my legs …

I can't move.

You are not supposed to.

I don't like it. I feel trapped.

You are trapped.

I don't feel in control.

You are in control. Just believe. You want to believe?

Yes, but –

Just as you tore me apart, I'm going to tear your face off. Remember, you said it would be wonderful. Just think how wonderful it would be.

I don't want you to –

It's not real. Imagine it. There cannot be any scope for doubt otherwise the world will always be inside you.

I don't want that.

Close your eyes … now imagine a world of possibilities … Imagine a world where you are no longer afraid, imagine that freedom … You, walking anywhere, running anywhere, in the fields, in the streets, in the woods … and nobody notices you. You become an irrelevance to other people. You become, like all the others, an irrelevance in this world.

Freedom!

Yes, freedom. Do you want it?

Yes, I do.

Do you really want it?

Yes.

You need to say it louder.

YES, I do.

I can't hear you.

YES, I DO.

Again.

YES, I DO!

I hear you. The world hears you. Keep your eyes closed. Now, turn your head to your left. What do you feel?

Nothing.

And now? Do you feel anything?

Your fingertips brushing my face ... From my temple to the front of my ear, down to my jaw-line and my chin. And back up again.

Believe ...

Your stroking is nice.

Believe ...

I believe.

Here, this is a nice area – the edge of your face, below your ear, just behind your jaw ... I am going to cut your skin with my nail ... just going to mark it slowly, scratching the surface.

Ow!

See, you now have some lovely scratch marks.

Yes, I believe ...

I'm going to go deeper into your skin, through the scratch marks.

Ow!

Moving my nails further in.

Ow!

And ... here ...

Ow!

I've pierced your skin with my nails and they really are under there.

Ow!

Just believe.

I believe.

Ready?

I am ready.

Just digging, pushing my fingers in deeper.

Ow! Argh! ow!! ... Your nails, they are hurting.

It has to be real.

Ow! ... Wait! ... I need to catch my breath.

... Ready?

Yes.

Here ... slowly ... gently ... my fingertips and nails are already under your skin and I'm just going to push my fingers further in behind the flap ...

Argh!

Just trying to get in ... under your face.

Argh! Argh!

I need to scrape my way under the muscles, so that I can get my fingers fully in. Using my fingers like a spatula, so I can hack my way in under your muscles

Argh! Argh!

It feels like your mask is stuck to your face.

Push your fingers in further. Push them in! ... Argh! Argh! Argh!

I am getting there.

I can feel your fingers scraping my muscles away from my bones ... Argh! Argh! Argh!

I am fully in there now.

Argh! Argh! Argh!

Are you ready?

I am ready.

I'm going to pull upwards and start ripping.

Do it. Do it!

Oh my god!

What's wrong?

Nothing – it's just so beautiful.

Can you see the truth?

Not yet. Your muscles and your tendons and your ligaments don't want to let go. They want to remain attached. Your face wants you to remain the same.

Force it! Pull harder!

I'm trying. I'm trying ...

Argh! Argh!

Your muscles are clinging on to your face and I am stretching your tendons.

Argh! Argh!

They don't want to let go ... Your face is being pulled to its limits.

Argh! Argh!

I am tearing your face off like I am tearing apart a loaf of bread.

Argh! Pull!

I can see the skin around your face slowly being torn and lifted.

Pull! Pull!

I am pulling!

Argh! You can do it!

Yes, I can!

What's that noise?

Your muscles, your tendons and your ligaments are all snapping now.

What a sound it makes! My face being ripped off!

Here's to freeing your face.

Rip it! Rip it!

Are you loving it?

It hurts so much. Do it faster, quicker!

I can see your skull and your right eyeball now that half your face is free.

I can see my face now. I can see the inside of my face with my right eye.

Turn. Turn your head the other way.

I'm turning.

Yes, it's easier to get at the other half off when you help.

Rip it, rip it!

It's stretching now ... Are you ready?

Yes.

Ow! OW!

I'm going to tug at it with some force.

Do it! ... Argh! Argh! Argh!

I've done it, I've done it!

Argh. Argh ... it hurts, it hurts.

It's beautiful: your face in my hands – dangling – it's beautiful.

Throw that face away. Chuck it!

Who am I throwing it for?

For all those people who stare at me.

You better look, then. I'm going to throw it over there to your left. You'd best say goodbye to the face with everyone's gazes on it.

Throw it!

There you go.

Goodbye, all you fuckers who ruined my life!

Look, look at it flying in the air.

It's like your –

Convex … Concave.

Outside. Inside.

Face outside. Blood and muscle inside.

Face then blood, face then blood.

Goodbye, horrible people.

Goodbye!

Goodbye, eyes!

I wish all those people's eyes were gouged out.

They have been. They were embedded in that face.

Fuck off you fucking eyes!

Your face has just hit the wall. Amazing that it sticks to it like that. Looks like your blood and muscles and whatever are clinging to the wall and projecting your face outwards.

It's a sad face.

And now it's slowly falling, still clinging to the wall.

It doesn't want to die.

Clinging on to life, but it's dying. Can you not see it sliding down?

It doesn't want to let go.

It's dying.

Soon there will only be the blood marks on the wall. It is real, right?

The blood is disappearing but it is real.

Die, you fuck-face!

…

Turn around and look at me now … Your face is still your face. It has healed. It is restored.

But my face is over there.

Look again … it's gone.

And now?

Let's do it again. This time I will do it quicker.

Do it again.

Look to your right this time. I'll do it the other way.

This time I'm not going to close my eyes.

You do what you want to do.

Rip it off fast this time.

I'll try my best. Who do you want to say goodbye to now?

To all those who did not want to touch me.

This one is for them.

Ow, ow!

Nails in.

Argh!

Struggling with these fingers. Hold on. Let me try this.

Argh! Argh!

Pushing my fingers in.

Argh! I can feel the force of your fingers inside my face.

Just a bit more.

Argh! Argh! Argh!

All in ... Ready to rip?

Ready.

Say your goodbyes when I rip it away ...

Good- ... Argh! Fuck! Argh! Goodbye! Argh!

Nearly there. Turn your head.

Argh ... goodbye ... you bastards! Fuck you, those who did not want to touch me ... Fuck off!

Pulling.

Hurry up, it's hurting!

I'm trying!

Try harder!

Something is not right.

Let me help. Let me turn my head

I've got it now! I've got it now!

Argh! Argh! Argh! Argh!

It's ripping!

Hurry up!

How I love pulling the skin off your face!

Argh! Argh!

I've done it!

It was painful!

Look how beautiful it is, dangling in my hands.

Throw it, throw it now!

Look at your face – flying the other way.

It's poetic, seeing it flying like that.

Like a ballet dancer pirouetting.

And those who do not want to touch me are dancing away.

Crashing, splattering against the wall.

It's clinging to the wall, looking at me.

Sliding down to the floor.

Look at the trail of blood that face makes on the wall.

It will disappear. They will disappear.

Fuck off!

That's right, you tell them!

FUCK OFF!

Again?

Again.

Want to wait awhile?

No. Again.

Look to your left.

This is for all the laughter and teasing.

In that case, I'm going to do my best.

Rip!

I'm ripping! I'm ripping! Make sure you throw out the laughter as well.

Faster! Get rid of those bastards!

I am ripping as fast as I can!

Argh! Argh! Fuck you, you cunts! Fuck your fucking laughter! Fuck you! Fuck you, you laughing, teasing bastards!

Fuck them! Fuck the lot of them!

Fuck off! Fuck off! Fuck off!

There you go … Flying with your face – the sound of laughter, pounding against the wall.

Yes. YES. *YES!*

…

That face looked tragic.

Laughter is tragic.

Hopefully it's dead.

Again. Do another one.

Face to the right, then.

Goodbye to all those people who avoided me.

Left.

Goodbye to people's false smiles.

Right.

Fuck off you little shits! Fucking little children, fuck off!

Left.

Goodbye to being alienated by the world.

Right.

Goodbye ... rejections.

Left.

No more. No more ... please ... I am too tired.

Yes, you'd better rest.

So many ugly faces ripped off me.

Look at me ... You are beautiful.

I don't feel it.

You're exhausted. You will feel better shortly.

...

Can I ask you a question?

Yes.

What did we just go through?

A barrier. A wall.

To be where?

To be nowhere but here.

IN A STRANGE PLACE

I heard you cry in your sleep last night.

Were you next to me?

Yes, but I left you after that. It seemed like you needed to be alone.

I was exhausted.

Why?

You ripped my face off!

I was tired too.

It was physically and emotionally draining.

Is that why you cried?

I don't know why I cried. All I know is that the world out there had finally penetrated through to my insides. I thought I had kept the world out but my skin could not resist it.

I have had other peoples' eyes burn across my body.

It's like that, isn't it? We want to be separate from others but we are in fact inseparable from them.

How do you mean?

The world out there: we live in it. The mess, the malaise, the sickness. People somehow seem to crawl onto and seep into our bodies ... I heard laughter again last night.

It wasn't me.

No, I know ... I think I must have cried because the laughter did not seem as venomous or humiliating as before.

You mean, like it was a relief?

Ripping off my face seemed cathartic. But I am no different and they are still there.

Yes, they are still there. There will always be people like that. We live in a world where there is sickness.

People are oblivious in what they do.

When I left you, I saw your face: it seemed so distant, so empty.

Can you not see that it has lost its memory of being itself?

I do appreciate why your face seems so distant – especially given the way you were treated; whilst other peoples' eyes burned into my body there was a notable absence of humanity to the way you were treated.

Friendly eyes do not burn.

No, they do not.

I dreamt something last night. The dream started off with laughter and ended with silence. The laughter seemed to diminish as the dream went on.

What was the dream about?

I don't quite know. Perhaps it was about the pain.

What was painful about it?

I saw my own face, like it was in a picture, perhaps a painting, I don't know. All I do know is that it was facing me. Just as I was looking away, I saw something in the left eye of the face, but when I took a second look I noticed that it was the eye itself. The inner corner of the eye then moved a little. It seemed to be moving downwards, dragging the skin between my eye and my nose down with it, as if it was stretching it. When the inner corner was at a forty-five degree angle downwards from where the outer corner was, the inner corner slipped, broke away from the skin, dropped like a pendulum, pivoting around the point of the outer corner of the same eye. Like a pendulum, it began to swing as it dangled there for a bit.

My right ear looked as if it was tearing itself away from that side of my head. The tear first appeared at the top of the ear where it meets my head, and slowly lengthened towards the bottom of my ear. My ear kept leaning further and further outwards as the tear worked further downwards.

Then my right eye became distorted, wavy, unrecognisable.

My eyebrows fell off: first one then the other.

My right cheek looked like it was melting, moving slowly downwards.

My left eye swung less and less until it stopped completely, at which point it fell off. As it fell, my nose shifted to a horizontal position, coming to rest on my left cheek. My right cheek continued to melt, drooping, dragging itself below my jaw-line. It pulled down on the middle of my wavy eye, stretching it from both its corners.

At the same time, my nose began to display earthquake-like cracks.

As my right ear broke away, toppling and falling, my melting cheek finally caused my right eye to snap away from its corners and slide into my cheek, being subsumed within it. My right eye no longer existed. It's seemed like the weight of the eye had caused my cheek to drop completely, leaving my face falling to the ground.

As it departed, my nose cracked into pieces and my left ear and mouth crumbled into dust, all of which also fell to the ground.

At the same instant, my right forehead pivoted on its left-hand side and swung ferociously, slamming into the base of my left cheek where my mouth once was. My cheek and forehead cracked into pieces, piling up on what was the remaining part of my lower jaw.

Then my jaw began to sag in the middle just like a structure with too much weight on it. It took some time before it snapped and the rest of my face fell to the ground.

I don't think there was anything left to laugh at.

Will you be honest with me? Did you take anything last night?

No, I did not.

They say our dreams have meaning.

Who are "they"?

Those people out there.

The ones who gaze at us?

Yes, those are the same people who want to interpret our dreams so they can look inside us.

To violate us again?

To invade our privacy!

You mean to control the meaning of our dreams.

Yes. But you must reclaim it. Tell me what your dream means to you.

My dream is a lived experience, just like my body is. When you hear about my dream, what do you think?

Do you want me to invade your privacy?

I want to understand your gaze, to understand your truth.

Just like the landscapes of our bodies?

Yes.

But my interpretation of your dream will not be the truth.

Your understanding of me is.

I think it is more important for you to understand your dream. Do you think the world finally got to you?

Are you asking me if I lost the battle?

Yes.

No. I was looking at my face – it wasn't my face; I was just looking at my face.

The world has penetrated you deeply.

Yes, but I don't think it was that.

If not the world, then you?

My face being ripped off was cathartic.

Then those masks are finally fading.

Yes.

It will take time.

I just thought of something: in my dream I was looking at my face, though it was not my face itself, but my face which I was looking at. There was a physical distance between me and that face.

And?

And there was a distance between you and me when I woke up: you were there and I was here. Why were you there?

I couldn't get to sleep last night.

Were you worried about anything?

I was restless. I couldn't stop thinking and feeling things.

Were you thinking of me hacking away at you with a machete?

Where do I start? It was scary …

My skin: it felt strange. Like it was itching, moving, burning and bubbling. It felt painful. My whole body was in pain. The more I rubbed my skin, the more agony I felt. When I touched my skin, it sent shockwaves down my nerves … bringing tears to my eyes. The pain inside was angry, it could not get out and shot its torment into my mind.

I could not get to sleep as the pain was all over me. My flesh seemed like it was creeping, rumbling underneath with hurt, with the lies, with the world. My skin prickled within, intolerably, unabating, reminding me of the sickness out there. When my skin was burning with rage, I felt my flesh cry – a sweat broke out on me.

Then dampness took over. The coldness seeped through my veins, freezing my blood. My body felt wet all over. I could even hear the dampness in my lungs, in my breath – a wheezing sound. The dampness spread to my brain. It was cold inside my skull. I could feel it closing in. I got up at that moment, just before it consumed me completely, and that's when I heard your cry.

I thought you were having a bad dream.

It sounds like you almost died.

I wasn't even asleep.

What were you thinking about at the time?

I was angry at the brutality of our lives, the brutality of trying to get rid of our pasts, and that even in the uncontrollable thoughts I was having there was a certain degree of brutality being inflicted on me.

Having listened to you and having said what I just said, it seems our minds tell us that there is only one way to understand such brutality, and that is: physically.

Why couldn't I simply be tired after what we just went through? Why did I have these thoughts?

I don't want this any more! I don't want the brutality! It is all encompassing. They, that malaise, that mess out there – it is suffocating.

There is no world of I and Them or You and Them; perhaps there is one of You and I or Us and Them.

The distance people showed me – in their eyes, their voice, their unwillingness to touch, their avoidance – that distance between them and my body and my face permeated my skin, and to survive the constant onslaught of that malaise I had to withdraw myself from my skin, which was what took the pounding – distance myself from that penetrated dermal barrier. The intrusion of the world was too much and I had to retreat to survive. I used this dermal barrier to create a "front", what you have highlighted to me as a mask. As long as I had that "mask" I wanted the world to reject that and not me, which, unknowingly, the world had penetrated.

You and I have a lot more in common than you think. We both dislike that sickness. We are both engulfed by it. We have both had to survive, somehow.

How did you survive?

I have memories of a time before my scoliosis. You never had that time. Ever since those memories stopped being created, I've distanced myself from the world out there, but I needed you to cut out my spine and tear out my ribs for me to realise certain things. I felt a little bit freer when you asked me to externalise that sickness which wove itself into me. My body is not so distant to me now. It feels a little bit more comfortable to wear.

It is true, then, that it is Us and Them.

It is only true if we occupy a shared space together, otherwise it will be You and I and Them.

In a Candlelit Room

I was hoping that we could now share a space together.

Will we be away from the madding crowd?

It will be We and Us.

What use is a shared space when you and I are still distant from our bodies? We will be "there, but not quite there": two objects sharing a space.

I think we need to get in touch with our skins, with the edge of our bodies – the surface of our own "objects".

But I have been in touch with your "surface".

Yes, but you seem deeper in yourself than I am. Touching someone and being touched are two different things.

You have touched me as well.

Yes, but you remain detached from the surface of your skin. The distance you describe is still there emotionally, physically and psychologically. Imagine if "You", the inner "You", and the boundary that is the edge of your body are one and the same – would you be an object? Would you be "there" and "not quite there"? You and I could be "there" in that same space.

What happens if I am overwhelmed by it all?

Do you see a sickness in me?

No.

What do you see in me?

Somebody nice.

Why would you not want that niceness?

Fear.

Or trust?

What's the difference?

Do you fear me?

No.

It's just that you don't know how to trust someone. I am still part of the world that is out there. Yet you have been naked here with me. How much more trust must I show you to convince you to pull you away from thinking too much about what is going on inside you? Can you let the "niceness" touch the edge of your body?

...

You look so sad.

I feel it is getting all too much.

Why?

You are beautiful.

But I am not.

Your beauty, your face, so close up, so intimate, is like other people's gazes that overpower me. It scares me ... I feel out of control. It's like I have waited a long time for it and now I cannot understand why it frightens me.

First times always frighten people. Usually in silence.

It cannot be that. I have wanted it for a long time. In my head it is beautiful, but my body is repulsed by it.

I was once like you.

How did you overcome it?

I just closed my eyes, to shut everything out, and tried to understand my body, what it was feeling, the sensations I needed to connect with. I did not want my

151

mind or emotions to judge what my body was experiencing – you see, it was other people's judgements that made me uncomfortable with myself. I just wanted to experience being touched unconditionally and not for an ulterior motive or purpose.

That's what I want – to be comfortable in my own skin.

For me it only lasted a short time before those horrible boys got their way, but I am aching for that freedom again.

It would be nice to experience that.

But you can. We can. We can be scared together. The problem is that time is not endless.

I know, I know … Shared spaces mean touching, don't they?

Yes.

Can we do it slowly?

Yes … Let me touch you gently. Not for any reason other than for you to reconnect with the edge of your body, to get in touch with your skin. I will touch you in a non-threatening way. I won't touch your sex. I won't touch your chest. I won't touch you to arouse you and I don't want to touch you for my titillation. I want to touch you so that you can trust your own body to experience different sensations, to experience touching in an unconditional way – a distance of zero between you and your body.

You won't touch me there?

Your sex and your chest can be off limits. If you want, just say "Stop" when you feel uncomfortable with anything, and I will stop.

Off limits?

Yes ... and you can stop any time.

What do you want me to do?

Just lie there. Close your eyes. I will tell you what I will be doing, where I will touch you. All you have to do is not say a word and simply experience your body.

You will stop if I ask you to?

Yes.

...

Let us start with your back first – it will make you feel safer. Turn over and face downwards; I will sit to one side, with only my hands touching you.

I'm just going to start by stroking you gently on your neck ... downwards with one hand and then the other ... stroking you just a few times ... and now I'm going to continue the stroking motion down to your shoulders ... this time using my fingertips along each side ... just approaching the outer edge of your shoulders.

I'm going to use a bit more pressure and will use the palm of my hands ... working inwards across your upper back ... working my way to your spine ... a little less pressure now ... dragging my hands one after the other down your spine ...

Using the back of my hand now to work my way back upwards, along your spine ... across and outwards to your shoulders with the palms of my hands and adding little bit more pressure ... my whole hand including palm and fingers now surrounding each arm ... squeezing more firmly on your upper arms, then with less pressure over your elbows as I move downwards ... firmer again on your forearms ... to your wrists ... releasing ... now back up your arms with the back of my hand ... to your shoulders and inwards, working my way gently, stroking with my fingers ... tapping my fingers down your spine ...

Now I am using the heel of my hand to move to the sides of your waist ... my fingertips travelling down to your backside ... twisting my hands so that I can use the backs of my fingers as I move inwards over your bottom ... then over and towards the top of your backside ... Dragging the back of my fingers back down over your bottom ... now using the backs of my hands and adding more pressure, downwards over your legs ... gently over the back of your knees and more firmly again towards your feet ... putting my forearms across and going back up along your legs ... skipping the back of your knees ... to your bottom again ... now back to my palms and pressing a bit harder ... upwards to the top of your backside ... now towards the outer part ... less pressure now ... to your sides ... and upwards to your underarms ... tapping my fingers as I move to the centre of your back ... stroking downwards along your spine, one hand after the other, a few times, slowly ... letting the pressure fade.

Keep your eyes closed. Turn around now so that I can touch your front.

...

Relax and notice the sensations now at the front of your body ... Just remember I won't touch you where I said I would not, and you can say stop any time. Just connect with the edge of your body.

Let me describe what you are doing this time.

You don't have to.

But I want to. I want you to understand that I am connecting.

Your feelings should be for yourself. It's about absorbing and understanding rather than expressing.

I won't tell you about my feelings; I just want to describe what I think you're doing. My body needs to confirm its understanding of what is going on.

Just don't tell me what you feel or how it is making you feel. Tell me what you understand.

I can feel your fingertips touching the base of my throat ... They're moving outwards along my collarbone ... Your hands are gently feeling the hardness of the bone ... moving towards my shoulders ... pressing firmly now with the palms whilst moving over my shoulders and down my arms ... back up along my arms using the backs of your hands and fingers ... sliding your fingers then your palms between my arms and my body ... firmly, now, down my sides ... to my hips... You are moving inwards to my abdomen and are using less pressure ... circling my navel with alternate hands ... pressing down gently with the pads of your fingers ... and outwards from the base of my abdomen using the heels of your hands, very gently, to the sides of my hips ... dragging your fingers down the sides of my legs ... past my knees ... to my ankles ... lightly resting your palms on them – holding the front of my feet and ankles ...

Now you're moving upwards, gently, with your palms, along my legs, skipping my knees and back down to my lower thighs ... the backs of your fingers on the fronts of my thighs ... working your way upwards to the top ... and ... outwards to my hips, tapping your fingers as you go ... back to the base of my abdomen ...

Circling my navel again now with your hands ... and now to my sides and upwards with the backs of your fingers ... to my shoulders ... upwards and over ... changing directions, tracing inwards along my collarbone, and coming back to where you started ...

You can open your eyes now.

I –

No, there is no need to share anything. Just absorb the experience: understand what your body felt.

Was I correct in describing how you were touching me?

It is not about being right or wrong. It is about understanding, being comfortable and attuned to the edge of your body.

I think I understand what my skin was experiencing.

And by focusing on that did you notice anything else?

I did not notice anything else.

Did you notice me?

No. Neither did I notice any eyes or judgements. It was just about sensations. I did not think about anyone else. Is that what it means to be free – free from the past?

Perhaps … But you only know about receiving. What about responsibility?

I don't understand.

Can you take responsibility for connecting with others, to understand not only the sensations that you feel when someone touches you but also the sensations you may feel when touching me?

But I touched you when you were lying next to me.

You were describing my body, not sensing it. Each description was a revelation, a judgement, in the way you described me. It was superficial, not a real understanding of what goes on inside, just something we were trying to make sense of. Here, now, you said you "think you understand what your skin was experiencing". It tells me that there is still a distance and that the distance is not about a one-way direction – something that you receive – but a two-way interaction – a relationship with the edge of your body.

Would you like me to touch you?

Yes.

What if I do not want to touch some parts of you?

It is all in your control. I am not going to judge you. I also do not want you to judge me. My body is not off limits to you. You take responsibility, but I do not want you to arouse me, nor do I want you to touch me with any other purpose than to note what sensations you can feel with your fingers and hands.

I am not sure if I could touch you on your sex.

You don't have to.

You sit up against the wall with your legs open and I will sit between them resting my back on you. That way, you can explore me without the pressure of my body staring at you.

And my eyes?

Close them when I am resting on you. Let your hands explore. I may guide you occasionally, by placing my hands on top of yours and directing your hands, but I won't force you. You can listen to my hands, or not.

Can I say "Stop"?

You can say "Stop". I can say "Stop". We simply stop then.

I did not say it when you were touching me.

Did you feel threatened?

No.

Perhaps that's why you did not say it.

But now I will think too much about where and how I touch you.

Just remember to focus on texture, the form, the temperature, and not where you are touching me. If I brush the back of your hand downwards, you should move your hands slower. If I brush the back of your hand upwards, move faster. If I tap your hand, then be firmer. If I tap it twice, be lighter. I will guide you. You do not need to think about how you are touching me. You just focus on what you are sensing.

That has taken a lot of pressure off already.

Remember: no purpose. Just understand the edge of your body.

Let me sit up, then … Come and sit here.

Will you be okay if I sit with my back on you?

Yes.

Let me huddle in.

....

Could you move slightly? Your shoulder and rib hump are pressing down on me and hurting me a bit.

Sorry!

No, don't be. I am sure if I put my weight on you, you would not be comfortable.

It's okay. I am not offended.

That's better.

When you close your eyes, tell me what you feel with your hands, and I don't just mean what you touch.

Will you close your eyes?

I will close my eyes.

…

I can feel you breathing.

I can feel you as well. Your chest is moving gently.

Close your eyes.

They are! Are yours?

Yes ...

I can feel the side of your shoulders with my hands and fingertips. They are soft ... your skin is smooth. I can squeeze your muscles gently like this ... and let go. At the tops of your shoulders, my fingertips feel a hardness – it's a bit bony ... it is softer as I go along the front of your shoulder – there's more muscle here.

Moving downwards I am surrounding your arm with my hands and fingers. Your arms feel softer, less firm than your shoulders ...

I can feel your elbows in the palms of my hands – hard and bony. At the front of your elbow there is a slight dip.

Just changing my touch to feel your outer forearm with the back of my fingers ... moving down your arm to your hand ... your wrists seem tough and hard ... changing my touch to use the pads of my fingers, and I can now feel the back of your hands – at times it is soft and at times hard. Your bones are like ridges and there are some lumps that feel like your veins.

Sliding my fingers between yours, I can feel your bony fingers surrounding mine – your finger bones to the side and in between my own fingers as they pass over yours ... I can feel the hardness of your nails ... it's different to sensing your bones: there is no skin covering them; they feel different in the palms of my hands.

Sliding my palms and fingers over yours ... my hands are in your hands ... It is less smooth here, not rough, just less smooth. I feel the heat in your hands ...

Stroking your inner forearms upwards towards your elbows ... lifting your elbows and your arms upwards, so that I can feel your inner upper arms ... cupping my hands around your upper arms and sliding down to you to your underarms, changing to my fingers ... My fingers feel some stubble here; it is also a bit clammy – just caressing your underarms now.

Using the back of my fingers now, to go under and around to the back of your shoulders, changing to the front of my fingers to go over your shoulders … pressing down firmly on your upper arms to lower them.

With my right hand I am reaching over you to your left shoulder, and I'm following the line of your collarbone. I can feel the thin, round bone. The skin over it is loose. There are dips to either side, above and below … Dragging my fingers along it – your collarbone seems to be further up your body as I move towards your throat …

Near your throat the dips shallow out below your collarbone, and I feel the firmness of your sternum and a softness, with very little resistance, just above the base of your throat.

Taking my hand away and reaching with my left hand to your right shoulder … following your collarbone inwards – this one is much higher than on your left side. The dips on the underside of your collarbone are deeper on this side … It seems to shallow out somewhat. It is not as smooth or level a transition to your sternum on this side …

Moving to the centre of your throat … resting my palm on your sternum, my thumb to one side of your throat and my fingers on the other … My palm is resting on something solid; my thumb and fingertips are resting on the something softer on either side of your throat. The middle and top of my palm is resting over the bony structure of your collarbone, whilst further down, to the outer and lower part of my palm, there is the softness, almost the hollowness, of your upper chest. There is warmth around your throat. I can't feel any heat on your upper chest.

I can feel your hands upon mine now and your fingers entwining with mine … You are dragging my hand back downwards … I do not think I want to go there yet.

I just want you to feel the cavity where my breast sits.

162

I can feel the dip from the middle of your chest to your right breast … The dip is hard and bony like your collarbone …

I'll move back to the centre of your chest …

Using all my fingertips, moving towards your abdomen … and outwards, bringing my hands now to the sides of your body, which are much softer ... moving both hands down your hips … my left hand rising over your body to the curvature over your raised left hip ... I can feel the hard edges of your left hip. Your right hip seems flat and in line with your abdomen … moving both my hands inwards…

I feel your fleeting touch on the backs of my hands ... pressing slower, but firmer, with both hands meeting in the centre just above your pubic area ... and outwards to your upper thighs, loosely gripping and then surrounding them … Your skin is soft here … Releasing and stroking your thighs upwards with my fingers ... raising my hand so that my fingertips glide back up over your hip …

Your hands are guiding me inwards again ... pressing down my hands to feel under your navel with the pads of my fingers … soft ... gentle ... and now working my way back out to the side of your body …

You are guiding my right hand upwards to your right breast … It is soft and firm ... It's a lot smaller than the other breast … Your hand is telling me you want me to keep my hand there? ... Now you want me to squeeze firmly? ... Am holding it there ...

I am going to move my hand back to the side now ... I think that is all I can do for now.

Are you okay?

Yes.

Are you sure?

Yes.

I do not want to know how you felt. Keep that to yourself. It is about you reaching out of yourself and being integrated with your touch; to know that no one is being judged by you when you touch them. I felt your fingers and hands across most of my body but now I am going to turn around so that you can touch my calves, ankles and feet – I need you to do this for me, to complete your exploration of me, as I do not want to feel half done, to feel that the top half of my body, where I have had the most problems, is the only area you are going to touch. I do not want to feel exploited like a circus act. Touch me where I have no problems, please. Touch my legs – don't leave me lopsided.

Okay.

You stay in that position; I will lie down in front of you.

Will you lie sideways beside me?

No.

Then how?

I will be on my back, my body between your legs and my legs bent over yours, so that you can access my lower half ... Just carry on as before.

Same rules?

Same rules, same conditions.

Are your eyes closed?

Yes.

Just placing my hands over your upper thighs ... my palms and fingers over the front of your thighs, my thumbs on your outer parts and my fingers towards the inner ... pressing firmly ... I can feel your muscles rolling in my hands as I move them upwards towards your knees ... Now sliding them back slowly downwards towards your upper thigh ... out towards the outer side of your upper thigh ... around and under ... changing the position of my hands so I can feel your thighs with the back of my fingers ... clenching my fists so I can press firmly against your muscles as I move upwards – your muscles are firm, but soft enough for me to slide upwards.

Unclenching and squeezing my fingers into the space between your calves and the back of your thighs, behind your knee – it's a bit clammy here ... Pulling, tugging my fingers out from there ... I think you are using your leg muscles to keep them there ... They've escaped now ... Walking my fingers from the outer side of your knee over the top and to the front.

Using my forearms to move down your legs. My inner forearms first ... sliding down your shins, touching you with my middle forearms and then lower forearms, and as I slide downwards, feeling your shin bone pressed against me ... Reaching down now with my fingers over the top of your feet ... touching you fleetingly upwards along your feet ... and downwards.

Sliding my hands under them and clasping your ankles in my hands ... my palms over your Achilles' heels ... thumbing your hard bony ankle ... pressing firmly with my thumb, tracing your ankles, rising up and then down over the other side of the bumps ... Using less pressure, I am semicircling back and forth around the lower half of your ankle ... letting go slightly and moving to the base of your calves, squeezing and relaxing as I move upwards ... Using my thumbs and fingertips to clasp your calves ... squeezing and letting go as I move upwards ...

Moving my hands to be around the front of your knees, touching you with my fingertips ... now moving and cupping my hands around your inner thigh, as my fingers slip between your legs ... sliding downwards to your upper thigh ... squeezing and then letting go of your upper inner thigh ... dragging my hand back upwards to your knee ... sliding down again, increasing the pressure as I move, squeezing and letting go of your upper inner thigh.

Touch me there. Feel the edge of my body. It's all in your control.

You are hungry for my pain, aren't you?

I am hungry for your affection. Perhaps my "chewed-up toffee" needs acceptance also.

It's soft ... moist.

Shh, you mustn't say anything!

But I want to.

Tell me what you touch, then. Tell me what you think.

...

It's not what I thought it would be like.

What did you think it would be like?

I don't know ... It's soft, like my lips, but there is very little resistance. My lips are not perfect: they are raised on one side; there is a cleft. Your labia are gentler, and, in this corner, here, at the top, this little lump, hidden away – your clitoris seems to be shy.

Lift up the hood.

Yes, I can see it now ... I don't know which lips to stroke – the inner or outer ones.

Touch both. Start outside and work towards the middle.

I am using my thumb to slide down your left labia. It seems to be swelling.

It's okay, there is nothing for you to worry about.

Gliding towards the bottom and upwards on the right one ... and back to the top. Your inner labia hang out slightly.

Try to understand them with your fingers.

Just rubbing them between my fingers and thumb. Does it hurt?

No.

Yes … they are softer … And there is more of them. It is difficult to differentiate between the two sides of them here at the top … Further down, they easily open up.

Open them. Have a look.

No.

That's okay.

I would like to stop now.

Hey, that's okay, too. Let me get up and sit beside you.

…

I want you to know that it isn't you.

You don't have to explain. You have to realise what you have achieved.

I reached out and you are still beside me.

Yes, you reached out and gave something to me: you touched me without judging me. I received something that you gave of yourself.

And you did not run away.

No, because I want to be a part of your space.

How do you know so much?

I have been with others. I have experienced it when I thought there was no hope in my life. When there is no hope, you become aware of receiving, you become aware of giving and …

And?

And nothing.

No! And? … Truth and honesty, remember.

Yes, I know.

And?

I experienced it and, as I have said before, I was humiliated by it.

Yes, you told me that.

Humiliation makes you no longer trust the edge of your body … When I am here with you, I am also re-learning. Whilst you receive, I am learning to give again. And as you give, I also re-learn how to receive.

Why could you not share that with me before?

If you saw someone in greater pain, more vulnerable than you, would you take the lead even if it meant hiding your own fragility? I am just trying to find my way forward with someone I want to be with, that's all.

Yes, I want that too.

Why don't we face each other ... You and I can share this space together, rather than one of us being passive.

I would like that. When you are here I do not want to experience things by myself. I don't want it to be all about me and then all about you.

Why don't we sit facing each other, our legs apart so that they do not get in the way and we can be closer together – almost hugging one another.

Place your legs over mine, bend them over mine – it will give us some room between us.

That would be nice.

...

Look at me. We should close our eyes again. Let's trust our senses again. This time we will both be giving and receiving at the same time.

Let's not have the "off limits" rule.

Okay, but we mustn't get carried away. I want your body to know that giving and receiving at the same time are not things to be feared but something we must be comfortable with. Life is like that. The world is like that. We learn to connect to one another.

But people *are* the problem.

Yes, but they are not here, its just you and I in our own space – I am the Other. Let's see if we can interact with mutual respect – no more distance.

…

You placed your hands over my heart.

Your palm is over my chest.

Your hands are warm.

I can feel your fingers moving along my collarbone. You're tracing around my breast.

Are you following me? Your fingers are tracing around my chest … I can feel them on my nipples.

I like the way you are stroking my breasts.

You're toying with my nipples.

You've found mine.

I feel little bumps around the base of your nipples.

My nipples are sensitive.

You've gone to my face now.

I feel the warmth of your hands holding each of my breasts.

You're moving across my forehead, down to my cheeks, under my eyes …

Your hands are at my sides.

Your fingers are on my nose now …

Down to my waist.

Down to my lip. You're touching my lip, my scar.

Why have you opened your eyes?

You're touching my lip, my broken lip. There's a huge gap.

It's as one to me …

Why were your eyes open?

I just wanted to look at this beautiful face close up.

And?

*Let me put my hands on the either side of your face … Lean forward …
Kiss me …*

Did it feel funny?

No.

A split lip kissing you?

Why the tears?

I never thought …

*Shhh! … You're gorgeous… No? Come here, close your eyes. Hold me.
Let's start again.*

…

Your head is on my right shoulder.

*You're stroking my back, up and down, as if you were playing a guitar,
only in slow motion.*

The fingers of your left hand are moving down my spine.

Do guitars have little bumps like the edge of my spine?

Your right arm is on my other shoulder. Your left arm is holding onto my back.

Your right hand is passing over my rib hump – I can feel it travel across each rib.

I can feel your fingers in the crack of my backside.

You're moving up over my larger right shoulder blade.

Moving your right hand to my hips … touching my scars now.

They must've hurt you?

No. Only the reasons behind it did.

You've moved to the back of my head.

I want to touch your face.

Let's uncouple.

…

Your hands are on my midriff now.

Yes, and you are holding my face between your hands.

…

I am touching your stomach … Don't you feel anything? … How about here – the scars on your rib…?

Why are you silent all of a sudden?

You've opened your eyes again … you're staring at me.

I don't mean to.

Your eyes don't burn me … Does it bother you that I am touching your scars?

No.

Why are you looking down, then?

I …

I see … Why don't you kiss them, then? Kiss my breasts … I'll lean back.

You're guiding my hands down there.

I am just taking your hands over here, placing them behind my back so you can support me as I lean back ... I'll just put my hands around you again ... Try the left one first ... Close your eyes. It will be better ...

Mmm ... I can feel you at the top of my breast ... I can feel traces of your saliva ... You're all over my breast ... lips surrounding my nipple ... I like the gentle squeezing ... Again, please ... And again ... It's like a pulse ...

You've stopped ... You look lost ... Why are you looking at me?

Oh, I see. You don't need my permission ... just explore – use your tongue, it will be even nicer ...

Your warm hands are on me again, holding my breast ... I feel a firm squeeze ... I feel your wet tongue on the underside of my nipple ... You're moving it sideways and around my nipple...

My other breast is getting lonely now ... When you get there, you don't have to hold it. Try using your mouth and tongue.

This one is smaller.

I feel your lips around my breast, kissing me softly ... on my inner breast ... upper breast ... outer breast ... You have taken my breast inside your mouth ... Your tongue is pressing upwards on my breast ... sandwiching my nipple with the roof of your mouth ... holding me ... sucking me.

...

I could feel the hardness of your nipple in my mouth. My mouth felt better on this side ... Come back near me. You don't need to lean back any more.

Let's just carry on being together. Shall we close our eyes again?

Yes.

Placing my hands on your thighs.

You are stroking me.

Now I feel your hands on my thighs, sliding up and down them.

You are massaging my legs.

Your hands are squeezing my thighs firmly … moving down to my groin area … halting and retreating upwards… moving back down again … and up …

Your warm hands – stroking me around my pubic area.

You have moved to my lower abdomen – lightly, with your fingertips.

…

Give me your hands.

Our fingers are interlocked.

Let me place your hand on my heart.

I want to do the same with your other hand.

…

Your hand is warm and comforting.

So is yours … Can I touch you lower down?

Yes. Keep this hand here, though. Use the other hand and I will do the same … Place your hand under me so that I can feel your palm against my sex.

Your hand is over my sex.

Let's remain like this for a few moments … Your sex is pressing against my palm. I can feel it grow and get harder.

You're getting warmer and moister down there. Your heart is beating faster.

I can feel your hand pressing more firmly against my sex.

I can feel your palm against my erection and your fingers cupping me underneath.

I am not going to hold your sex just yet.

No, it's nice like this.

Let's wait a few moments …

Open your eyes.

…

What did you think of my disfigured lip touching you?

I didn't think anything of it. Your lips are nice and gentle … soft … beautiful … moist.

I am ugly!

You are not!

The world judges me by my face.

The world is not here. Just as you do not think about my scoliosis in these moments, what you just said did not even enter my head.

That's true, I did not think about you in that way when we were touching each other. The shape of our bodies did not exist.

…

Why don't you lie down on your back now? I am going to sit astride you.

What are you going to do?

I want your body to know that my chewed-up toffee is beautiful.

How?

I want you to lie down on your back so that I can sit astride of you. I want you to close your eyes so that you cannot see my sex. I will touch you. All you have to do is to understand the sensations in your body. I do not want you to be active at all.

I felt a bit aroused when we were touching each other.

I know. Be aroused if you want, but resist movement – be passive, keep your pelvis still.

What are you going to do?

I am going to touch you, that's all. Your body is on limits now if you want it to be so.

I do.

I am going to touch you with a part of my body that was "off limits".

Your sex?

Try not to think of anything but the sensations. I will tell you what I will be doing so that you don't feel any trepidation. Just focus on the bodily sensations.

Lie down on your back now and I will be astride and above you, supporting myself, so you can focus on my touch and not my weight.

…

I need you to put your hands out to the sides or above your head, as my hips and spine will start to hurt if I position my legs too wide.

Close your eyes.

…

Your pubic hair is tickling my chest.

How about now?

I don't know. Something is on me.

Something?

I mean your sex.

What about now?

You're moving it from side to side. I can feel it dragging. It's a bit wet … You're moving across to my nipple … You're over it … It feels like you are teasing it … Have you lowered yourself onto me, as I can feel something now?

Yes, I am just moving from side to side.

I can feel one of your lips folding over and being dragged one way and then the other. Whatever way you move I can feel the wetness of the other lip.

Just moving up and down now, so that your nipple can explore it all … Now your nipple is in my slit – I am surrounding your nipple.

I can feel it surround me.

Does it frighten you?

No. It just feels … different.

Horrible?

No … I can't describe it.

Okay, I'll go back in the middle now … I'm going to slide down over your abdomen – but I will need to manoeuvre myself first … Sliding now towards your hip … down to your thigh … to the side of your sex …

It's quite erotic there.

Going back up towards your abdomen up around your sex to the other side … Is it as "erotic" here as it was on the other side?

Yes.

Do you like me touching you here?

Yes.

How about now?

You're over my scrotum. It's ticklish.

How about now?

Your weight is on me.

Sorry – how about now?

You're at the base of my sex.

I'm just going to lower myself a little; I'll try not to put my weight on you.

Your sex is surrounding me – you're on either side of my penis.

Let me know if it's too much for you.

I feel aroused.

Yes, you are. I am, too … I am moving up and down along your penis … Slightly up first and then back down … further up, and back down … Nearly to the top, and back down … I'm going to go to the top and rest there …

Are you okay?

Yes.

Rubbing myself around the top of your penis now … I am going to use the tip of your penis to lift the hood of my clitoris … I think it's there now. Trying to rest my clitoris in the slit of your head.

It feels sensual. Powerful.

It's making your breathing shallower and faster.

Yes.

I think we should change positions now …

Can we stay here for a while?

Remember, it's all about noticing the sensations and getting used to my sex.

It felt good. It felt nice.

And the image in your head? Was it one of pleasure or disgust?

There wasn't any disgust behind it.

Did you feel any stigma experiencing this?

No, I was focused on my body, not the history of what other people have done.

Your sex, my sex, they don't know how to judge to each other.

No, they don't.

I want you to get on top of me now.

Do you want me to do the same to you?

No. I want you to explore me. I want you to know that despite everything that has happened to you, you can be active with me, active in being with this naked woman in front of you.

Use your sex as if it was your hand. You be in control of exploring me rather than me controlling you. My body needs to know that it can trust your sex.

Come on, let's change positions.

...

Put your arms above your head, my legs need to go either side of you.

Okay.

I am ready. Close your eyes. Tell me what you feel.

I can feel your scrotum in the middle of my chest … You're moving downwards … Now I can feel your hardness along the top of my chest … rubbing against me from side to side … You're using your penis to move towards my left breast, towards the nipple … It feels like you are teasing me … You're over it …

Your nipple is erect.

You're flicking my nipple from side to side … Now you're on top of it.

Putting your nipple in the slit of my head now … just moving my slit up an down over your nipple.

Moving away now … to the other side … I can feel your sex in the cavity on my right side … now moving over my breast … I can feel your sex move from side to side over my left breast … You're teasing my nipple by dangling your scrotum over it.

Do you like it?

Yes.

How about this?

You're moving your sex down my middle … I can feel your scrotum, and your hair, dragging down to my navel … You're moving it a around my abdomen … Moving to my left and onto my hip …

I can feel your hard sex slowly moving toward my waist … I can feel it moving across my waistline … and back across again … to the centre of my waist … and down, now, to my sex.

I need to move between your legs. If you open them, I can continue.

Here.

…

You're tracing your penis around my vulva.

Your vulva is becoming engorged.

Does it make you feel good to know that you can excite me?

Yes.

What now, then?

I'm just going to see if I can touch your clitoris.

You might need to direct your sex with your hands.

Yes, I will … How does this feel?

Wonderful … Are you sliding up and down my clitoris?

Yes, trying to.

I think you should stop.

Do I have to?

Yes, I want you to. Remember, it's not about us going all the way. It's about trust.

Yes, I'll stop.

No, no … Just rest your sex on top of mine …

Are you okay? Can you support yourself with your hands whilst you rest upon me? I don't want you to crush me.

I don't want to crush you.

Tell me when your arms begin to hurt.

I think you will know, because I might well fall on top of you.

I am sure you would tell me before that happened.

You know I will. You can see me now with my face hovering above your body.

Yes, I can, and I can see you looking at me.

How long do you want me to stay in this position?

All you have done is superficially touched my sex.

You saw my "chewed-up toffee" … You touched my chewed-up toffee and now you need to understand what lies behind the façade. Like I can understand what lies behind your façade – this beautiful face – the hurt, the distrust, the self-disgust, the loneliness. You have never really wanted to "know" – to be inside me. You have never really been free from that fear.

As I said before, you're in control now, and when you are ready, I want you to experience something sensual … Remember, I want you to experience <u>something</u>. We can make love later, but at this moment your sex needs to know how not to be afraid.

What do you want me to do?

I want you to enter me, step by step. A little at first. Then a little bit more. Then a bit more. I don't want you to start moving your hips, I just want your sex to understand what it's all about … Are you okay with this?

Yes, I am.

Enter me.

…

No, you're not there yet … No … Not quite … Here, let me guide you. Move your hips back slightly … I'm just holding you, here. This is my vagina …

Slowly, slowly, gently push in … that's it, that's it … Don't go all the way yet … And wait there, wait there and just hold …

Am I hurting you?

No, not at all … And pull out now …

Just going to guide you again …

Decide how far you want to go in and hold it … Remember, step by step.

How about this?

Yes, I can feel you. You're a bit deeper this time … How does it feel?

I can feel the walls of your vagina surrounding my sex; it's like it's holding me.

Do you like it?

It's a strange feeling … Let me pull out now.

Okay …

I want to try again.

This time, move a little bit further in.

How far?

I don't mind.

Guide me in.

Okay.

Your hands feel nice holding my penis when you're guiding me in.

Yes, I love your sex, too … Are you ready now?

Yes.

Enter me.

…

I'm inside.

Are you all the way in?

Yes.

Now, hold. Don't move your pelvis, just stay there and hold.

…

And let go.

I am out now.

Yes.

I like to guide myself in.

Okay … Have a look first so you know where to go.

I think I've got it.

Yes, you've found it. Push slowly … That's it – you're in now.

When I push in I can feel your sex pulling, grasping the skin of my penis.

Now, hold there for thirty seconds …

Okay.

…

I'm pulling out now.

Yes, I can feel you coming out.

…

Come and lie beside me now.

…

Why did I have to go in step by step?

I wanted to be accepted. To be respected and not feel exploited … Was my chewed-up toffee offensive to you?

No.

Did it remind you of anything?

No. I forgot about those horrible people and what they used to call me … I am confused now.

What do you mean?

Now I am not sure that my fear was ever about your vagina.

Too many people have hurt you. Too many people could not be trusted. That's why I think you put on those masks. I know I wanted to be with you, and you have since let those masks down one by one.

I think the hardest part was –

Was making sure your true, naked, complete self was not rejected!

How do you know?

I know, because that is what I felt in the past, and I did not want you to be humiliated like I was. I can't unravel all that has gone before, but your body trusts me now.

In a Shared Space

I'd like us to enjoy our space together.

So would I.

I would like us to talk as we share this space.

Talking will interrupt us.

No. I mean talk about what we are doing.

Like a commentary?

Sort of.

Why?

All our lives, people have looked at us with negativity. As we speak, our voices will observe what we do. It won't be your voice. It won't be my voice. It will be <u>our</u> voice.

Looking at ourselves?

Yes, describing something positive, something wonderful about us. No more glares, no more stares. What we will receive is not the distorted negativity of others but our beauty, the sense of how wonderful we are whilst knowing we will receive that beauty though our own observing voice – another voice that does not justify our existence from within but a justification from without – a voice looking at us.

It's kind of voyeuristic.

It's kind of erotic. Think about it.

I think I understand. Without that voice, it will be like you covering yourself up when you go out, or me, when I stoop to hide my face – we are being furtive, hiding in silence.

And by remaining silent we will still be hiding.

So if we share this space in silence, we will still be hiding.

Yes, but our commentary, our voice, will set us free.

No one else?

No one else. No one looking at us, just our voice.

Being free in a shared space.

Observing ourselves through the lens of our voice and not the lens of distortion.

Where do I start? What do I do?

Just speak as you move, as you do something.

You go first.

...

Stand in front of me ... Come closer, put your arms around my waist.

Like this.

Yes.

I can feel your hands around my waist, too.

I just want a good look at you.

You are staring at me.

So are you, at me.

You seem to be examining my face?

How can you tell?

Your eyes are moving from side to side.

You are doing the same to me – left to right to left.

I am?

Uh-huh – one eye to the other.

Are you looking at my lips now?

Your face is beautiful.

No. You are.

Let me touch you ... Your forehead is nice.

Your fingers are soft.

Close your eyes.

I can feel your fingers circling my left eye ... moving towards my ear ... down my cheek ... around my jaw ... and back up to my forehead.

I can feel your fingers running along the hairline on my forehead, moving from side to side.

You are at the top of my nose. Along its ridge, now, and down to its tip.

You're moving to my left ear and around the back. To my jaw again.

You are outlining my nostrils. First one then the other, longer one.

Your fingers are across my lips, moving left to right and then back again on the lower lip.

I can feel your palm resting upon my right cheek. Your thumb is outlining my lip, fingering the gap in it.

You're moving back to my forehead ... It's nice.

You are moving my hand away.

Yes. Put your hands around me.

You are tracing my lips with your nose, moving from side to side ... now with your forehead.

I can feel one hand behind my head. And your cheek on top of my head ... Let me nuzzle in under your jaw.

It's lovely to feel your face moving up and down my neck.

I can feel your warm hands on my cheeks, pushing me back.

Now I can see you again.

I can see you, too.

Kiss me.

...

Your kiss, it fires something in me. It's like some sort of sensual nerve pulse from my lips to my brain, and then it's like it's being transmitted, rushing back through my face, through my tongue and through to my mouth.

I could taste you in your saliva – it sent pulses down my body.

You closed your eyes when you kissed me.

I was trying to sense how delicate you might be.

Was I?

Yes.

Your pupils are dilated.

It may be because I can smell some pheromones seeping through your skin.

Perhaps you felt my heart beat through my lips.

Kiss me again.

I could feel your tongue touching mine. I could feel it brush my teeth. It felt like your tongue passed through them.

When you kissed me, I felt that your lips and my lips, in that instant, as we moved in towards one another, that your lips became my lips.

Kiss me again.

Close your eyes.

Wow! ... Kissing my eyes ... Down my drooping cheek ... A little moist trail of your saliva.

I like it when you kiss my forehead and the top of my head.

Let me look at you again.

I like it when you touch me gently with your fingers along my shoulders and along my neckline.

You are teasing me with your hands on my chest.

I have never seen you from this angle before, so close up. Never realised how nice your shoulders are.

Put your hands around my neck ... Kiss me.

Do you like it?

Yes – what are you doing?

I'm putting my legs around your waist. I'll kiss you if you hold me.

You're squeezing me too tight.

Support me, then.

I am.

Now I am taller than you. Kiss me.

Lean forward ...

I felt that my lips could not let go of your lips.

Yes, it was the same with me. I felt your lips pressing against mine, and when we parted they did not want to let go.

You see, that's a sign.

Of what?

That we belong to one another.

Although I think there just might be another sign saying something else.

Like what?

Like I can't hold you much longer.

Put me down, then ... What are you doing?

On my knees now.

You're tilting me backwards onto the floor.

What does that say to you?

It says that you deserve a kiss.

A kiss I will have.

*

It's nice to be lying down here naked, on our sides, facing one another. It allows me to stroke your face, to stroke this wonderful drooping cheek here on your right.

I like running my hands up and down your sides.

It feels different when you do that.

How do you mean?

It feels as if your fingers are reaching under my skin.

Look! They *are* under your skin. As I move my hand up and down your leg, it seems to sink into your body.

Where ...? Yes, I can see.

When I move my hand along your leg like this, my fingers sink into you, like I'm running my fingers through water, and the tips of my fingers that are within you I cannot see. It's as if your skin and the skin of my fingers above the surface of your leg are continuous.

It feels serene and sensual.

And when I lift my hand away from your leg, my fingertips reappear.

It doesn't matter. I think it is about how you and I feel, how much we believe in one another ... How much we want to share this space together. You are not hurting me.

There doesn't seem to be any extra resistance when I run my fingers up and down and through your legs.

My body welcomes you.

I can feel your fingers, too, dipping under and then on top of my face.

I am not putting on any pressure. But my fingers do sink in naturally with the movement of my hands. And they come to the surface with the flow of movement.

To feel someone's hand in the muscles of my drooping cheek makes me want to cry.

Painful?

No. Beautiful. It's like your hand is supporting it, giving it life, suspending it from the pull of gravity.

When I run my fingers along your lip, their tips bury themselves inside your lip. All I see is the lower part of my fingers and the surface of your lip; my fingertips are hidden.

The sensations there are much deeper. The signals from my lip to the rest of my body are much stronger.

I can feel your hand under the surface of my hip.

My palm is gliding upwards.

*Yes, it's inside my raised hip ... And now it is passing through it ...
now back on the surface of my skin .... Moving around to my back
and under my skin again, sandwiching between my skin and my muscles.
It's quite thrilling to feel such a deep touch rippling its way through my
body.*

I can feel your fingers moving down inside my throat.

I can feel your pulse ... it's passing through my fingers.

Now you are down to the base of my neck ... Your whole hand is
smoothing downwards across my chest. I can feel your palm
moving through my muscles.

I'm moving my hand away so that you can continue to reach me.

Your hands are passing under my arms and down to my sides.

Yes. Gently on the surface.

That feels nice.

Your hand feels much deeper as you run it down my back again.

I can feel your left arm sliding underneath me, through the side of
my body and on to my back.

Reach around me as well.

I can feel your hands gripping my back. Your lips seem to sink into my throat, kissing the outside of my windpipe.

I can feel your hand inside my back, inside the bones of my pelvis, at the base of my spine.

I can feel the brush of your head as you twist your scalp back and forth along the side of my jaw.

I can feel your hands slide along and through my spine, upwards, touching me where they tried to fuse my bone.

I can feel your glorious S curve.

That was wonderful!

My hand is on your neck now, back on the surface.

My left hand slides so easily down to the base of your throat, through your collarbone, over the ripples of your chest muscles and under your skin.

I can feel your hand under my skin, tickling my ribs as it rushes by.

Your fingers running down the surface of my scar.

Does it hurt?

No. It's massaging the scar tissue. It's lovely.

I can feel your hand on my skin around the back of my right hip.

That's nice. That's nice. Your fingers are turning me on, exploring the crack of my backside.

Yes, and your hands are now on *my* bottom; it's as if they have always been there. You are caressing me downwards and then lifting the muscles of my backside upwards from within.

I like it when you brush my anus … now your palms are going through my backside to the side of my body.

*

Is it true that we are here now, looking at each other?

Yes, we are! It's nice, isn't it?

Yes.

Stroking each other's arms.

And here, your shoulder.

You're pressing your hand against me. Do you want me to lie back?

Yes, so that I can have a good look at you.

...

Now I can feel the flat of your hand over my right breast, moving sideways across my chest to the other side of it and to the centre of my chest, moving downwards.

My hand sinks into your abdomen.

It feels like you are soothing my belly.

Do you like it?

Yes.

How about when I move my hands here?

I like it when your hand is over my left breast ... I can feel your fingers and thumbs squeezing it – oh, wow! Lifting my breast away from my body, holding it ... And now shaking it while it is suspended ... Putting me back ...

Your fingertips are tracing the outside of my breast.

And now my fingers are entering your skin, moving under your chest muscles.

Oh yes, I can feel your fingers coming through my muscles and now into my breast from underneath. Your thumb is on top, teasing my nipple.

Your nipple is hard.

And now you are lifting my breast from underneath.

My fingers are running through your breast.

I can feel your thumb and fingers coming together in pincer formation.

I have your erect nipple in between my thumb and fingers.

The sensations of your fingers on the underside of my nipple are like nothing I have felt before – it's so erotic. So many nerves being stimulated, the sensations coming all at once from the outside, with your thumb, and from underneath, with your fingers!

And does this little shaking and rubbing of your nipples help?

Yes – yes it does.

What about this, when I move to the other side?

That's nice too: my right breast was getting lonely.

My fingers seem to disappear into your breast as I brush across it.

I can feel the skin of my breast being pulled away by your fingers as you come out the other side.

And now, how about when I go back the other way?

I can feel them sinking, then moving through my breast, triggering all those wonderful sexual nerves as you pass through.

And as I leave, can you feel my hand working its way out of your breast to be on top of it?

Yes. I can feel your hands working themselves outwards to be on top of my breast ... And now your fingertips are following.

Now?

That's wonderful: your nails scratching my skin, claw-like, downwards over my breast to my abdomen. It's kind of sexy to feel your nails running through the top layer of my skin of my belly.

Is that your hands joining me?

Yes, I want to touch your abdomen.

I can feel your hand sinking in and then coming back out to the surface.

When I touch your scars does it bother you?

No. It feels sensuous when you do that.

Even when I touch them from underneath?

More so.

It's strange to see my hand gliding under your skin like that.

I can feel your hands there, moving through my muscles and through my ribs ... Up through my sternum and across my chest.

Your nipples are smaller than mine. Would you like me to do something with them?

Suck them.

Okay.

I can feel your tongue tracing my left nipple, your lips enclosing it ... and now the gentle suction as you hold my nipple with your tongue ... It feels as if my nipple is inside your tongue. With each movement of your tongue, I can feel my nipple being tugged at ... Your lips seem to be completely enveloping my nipple, and as you pull away those sensations increase: your lips and tongue also pull on my nipple as you release it.

It felt as if my tongue and your nipple were as one at one stage. But what do you want me to do with the other one?

Play with it.

Like this?

Yes.

…

I can feel your warm hands on my abdomen playing with my belly button.

You are dragging your fingers down my abdomen, dipping under my belly button, and coming back to the surface below it.

Over your sex.

I feel your fingers brushing around and over my sex … enveloping and surrounding my scrotum; the heel of your hand resting on the top side, your fingers on the underside, slowly sinking and closing in, gently pressing …

You are releasing me, moving your hand back up again, halting and then rolling your palm down and over the surface of my scrotum. Your fingers are reaching down to the underside again, touching me between my anus and scrotum. I feel your fingers pushing in, entering me in that area.

Yes, my fingers have dipped inside you there, and I am trying to massage you from within.

I can feel the reverberations of your fingers in the tip of my penis.

And now I am pulling my hands back up, moving it through that area to inside your scrotum … in between and now surrounding and cupping your balls, one by one. First the right and then the left one.

I can feel the clasp of your fingers surrounding each one, pressing down gently, slowly submerging into them, arresting and emerging from them, with each to and fro rolling action of your fingers as you play with me.

I can feel that your sex is hard as I move my hand back upwards.

Yes, I can feel your hands passing through it … It stimulates me further. It feels intense.

There's more resistance. It must be the volume of blood engorging your sex.

You are causing ripples to travel through my sex; each ripple excites me from within.

Are you pushing my hand away?

No. I'm just reaching down towards your sex. I want you to feel what I feel.

That would be nice. Let me move my arm away.

How about now?

Yes, your hand is forging its way under my skin and down through my abdomen.

And now I'm lifting it out from your body to rest on top of your sex.

Yes, I can feel your hand on my sex.

It's warm.

It knows you are there.

I can feel the softness of your sex.

Your finger is pressing between my inner lips.

I can feel your inner lips around my finger, drowning it, trying to hold it in place.

I can feel your finger sliding up and down between my labia.

Your sex is lubricating itself.

It wants more.

What about now?

I feel two other fingers, each between my inner and outer labia, the inner lips gently being squeezed between your fingers as you move up and down with your hand.

It feels like your outer lips have also trapped my fingers, bracing them in.

Your fingers are lifting, passing through them, and your whole hand seems to be cupping me now.

I can feel the heat of your sex.

I can feel your hand submerging itself, sinking into my sex, and now moving upwards, escaping from my sex through my abdominal muscles, rising and pulling away from my body, stretching my skin as you leave my body.

Moving to your inner thigh. Would you like me to focus on you here?

Yes, the sensations are wonderful there.

Spread your legs so that I can reach your thighs better ... that's it.

That's nice ... I can feel your hand on my inner thigh.

I am squeezing your right lower thigh between my thumb and fingers, and as they sink in, I am squeezing them from within your muscles, sliding through them, through your upper thigh and down towards your sex.

It's like an undercurrent coming to my sex, sweeping my nerves as you get closer, exciting my sex as the current passes through it, getting stronger as your fingers, then palm, then the heel of your hand moves through it.

And now past your sex and moving upwards, away from it, onto and up the other thigh, submerging and emerging, then back down again.

I can feel the heel of your hand tugging on my sex muscles as you move through it again, your trailing fingers strum across, up and away from my sex, pulling my sex muscles from within ... And now I can feel the second wave of your hand coming down my leg, using a pulsating action on my muscles: squeezing them and relaxing them repeatedly as you move further down.

My hands submerge inside your thigh muscles as I squeeze and then float to the surface of your skin as I release.

The rhythm of your hand movements relaxes me and excites me at the same time. I have pulsating sensations within my sex.

And now upwards on the other thigh.

You skipped me! You tease. You skipped my sex.

Anticipation!

Yes, yes.

Do you like me touching you here?

Yes, that pulsating rhythm is wonderful.

Your sex has deepened in colour.

Put your fingers inside me and stimulate my clitoris with your thumb.

Like this?

Yes. Use your rhythmic action.

Like this?

That's it!

As I move my fingers in, I am moving my thumb from the top of your vagina, upwards, in between your inner lips, towards your clitoris, rolling my thumb over it and then travelling back down, back to the top of your vagina and partially withdrawing my fingers from it as I roll my thumb back down.

And again ...

In ... Out ...

Again.

Your skin is flushing.

Again.

Your breathing has speeded up.

Again.

The muscles in your stomach, in your body, seem so tense.

Again ... In ... Out ...

I am squeezing as I move my hand downwards so that I can grab your sex, gently pressing it between my thumb and fingers as I move each time.

Yes.

I can feel your body pulse in your sex – it's increasing.

Yes.

Letting go of your sex from between my fingers now, as I move my hand upwards, so I can roll over your clitoris.

I can feel your fingers inside me.

Your nipples are so erect and your clitoris is retreating behind its hood.

Keep doing this until I say.

Your vulva is swelling.

Keep going ...

In ... Out ... In ... Out ... In ... Out ...

Stop! Stop! Stop!

It's okay! What happened?

I don't want to come just yet. I want to taste your sex first.

Your sex has given me sticky fingers.

It's because you turned me on.

And watching you has turned me on.

I can see that.

You were on the edge.

Yes, I was.

Can I kiss you?

No ... I want to kiss you!

Well, I shall lie here on my back waiting for it, then.

One for your forehead ... One for your nose ... Another for your lips ... This one for your chin ... Under your chin ... These three for your throat ... One for your chest ... And your heart ... For your ribs – either side ... This for your abdomen ... And now for your navel.

That one was a sloppy, tongue-based one.

This one is for below your navel ... This one for the tip of your penis ... For the shaft ... For your scrotum ... The left one ... The right one ...

I can feel your tongue running upwards from the base of my penis ... to its tip. I can feel your tongue reaching inside my penis near its base and slowly emerging to the surface of my skin as you push upwards to the tip, tickling my frenulum just before you get to the head.

Open your legs and let me sit between them ... so I can access you better ...

...

Now close your eyes.

I can feel both your hands on my chest, sinking in as you press down and drag them down my body.

I can feel the differing densities of your muscles and your bones as I move downwards, lifting my hand away from your body as I approach your groin.

I feel your fingertips surfing back upwards, across my skin, and your hands upon my chest again.

Stroking downwards.

Your hands are firmer this time.

I am moving them past your groin to your thighs and knees.

I can feel your hand travel through my muscle to my knee, through it and then out … The backs of your fingers now, smoothing my skin as you move up my thigh.

I can't see the tops of my fingers. It is if the tops of my fingers are within your body, and the surface of your thigh and the skin at the tops of my fingers are as one.

It feels like a wave running along my thigh.

And now?

Your palms and fingers on the upper part of my inner thigh ... Oh, yes ... that pulsating action!

...

See this area here?

Where you are touching me?

Yes, the area between your scrotum and your anus – it's called the perineum. Do you know why it's special?

No?

That's where your penis starts from, that's where the base of it is ... and I'm going to massage it.

I can feel your hands resting on my upper thighs now and your thumbs reaching inwards to my perineum, stroking me in circular motions, one after the other, from my anus to my scrotum ...

Yes, my thumbs are circling on both the left and the right, alternating, at the same time.

Circling whilst moving upwards ... and then downwards ... Now I can feel the pressure of your thumbs pressing into me, like there are pressure points there, entering me and then lifting themselves out, only to sink in again in a different spot nearby ... Oh, wow! I feel the sensuous signals travel from the base, where you are, to the tip of my penis, every time you press.

And your tumescence is getting bigger and stronger every time I press. I can feel the blood rushing in ... I'm going to grab your penis with my left hand and I'll keep palpating your perineum with my right hand.

I can feel your thumb on my frenulum and your fingers behind the head. It feels erotic when you squeeze the head between your fingers and thumb and then gently release it.

My thumb disappears inside your penis when I press.

I can feel it from inside as you squeeze. I can feel your fingernails triggering the nerves in my frenulum from within ... And the rhythm of your squeezing is in harmony with the palpations of your fingers on my perineum ... It feels if my whole sex is being stimulated at once.

How about now, when I press my fist gently, instead of using my fingers, onto your perineum?

You've stopped squeezing!

Yes.

I can feel your fist pressing and then gently submerging itself in my perineum, exciting me as you shake and rock my whole penis from the base to its tip in unison.

…

I'm just going to move my hands away now.

I can feel your fingers under my scrotum now. They seem to be entering me. Each set of fingers under each of my balls, moving in a circular motion.

Tantalising your sex.

Yes, it is.

What about now?

You are stroking the upper side of my balls with your thumbs ... It feels like my whole body is in a state of tension, yet relaxed at the same time.

When I look at you and I see the flush on your body – that difference in your face and your body between tension and relaxation – it excites me. It turns me on.

Even if I open my eyes, they cannot stay open for long, I have to close them.

I am just going to place my left hand around the top of your penis.

I can feel you moving my skin further down as you drag your hand down around my penis.

My fingers and thumb look like they are an appendage attached to you; your skin merges with mine, and as I move my hand down your penis, your skin is being pulled back with the downward action. Is it too tight, are you in pain?

No. Your hand seems to know the extent of the needs of my sex …
Slide back up.

Like this?

Yes. Down again.

Up and down.

Up again.

And down … This time I am just resting my hand at the base.

I can feel your thumb and index finger ringing the bottom of my penis.

I'm taking my right hand and surrounding your penis, just above where my left hand is.

I can feel your right palm resting on my penis and your thumb and fingers encircling me, with the thumb and index finger of your right hand resting on top of your left thumb and index finger.

Moving my right hand upwards along your shaft.

It's like a fleeting touch.

Yes, I'm not squeezing, grabbing or pressing as I move upwards – just teasing with barest of touches.

It feels like you're trying to stretch me.

That's what teasing is about.

You're moving back down ... and up again ... Down and up ... Down and up ...

And now I am tracing my right index finger underneath and all the way around the rim of your head ... First one way and then the other ...

It's electrifying!

Just like your fingers in my vagina.

...

I can feel your thumbs now on either side of my frenulum, just below the head. The first thumb is moving sideways onto my frenulum, and as it moves backwards I can feel the other thumb moving inwards towards my frenulum to replace the other thumb.

First one way, then the other. One way, then the other ... And some little circular motions at the same time ...

It's wonderful. It's wonderful.

Squeezing your frenulum … Just rubbing and stimulating the head.

Wow!

The veins of your penis are so pronounced. I can see that your scrotum is engorged and elevated.

Yes, I feel so much … pleasure.

Just changing positions now.

…

You're covering the head of my penis with your lips. I can feel them curling over onto the underside of the rim … and your wet tongue is playing with my slit … It feels like your tongue is opening it up, dividing it as you move along it, only for it to close in behind your tongue after you've passed through … I feel the wetness all over the head …

Your lips are moving further down … And your tongue is pressing against my frenulum. Now flicking it … And it's moving to the underside of the rim of the head … as far as your tongue can go one way and then back around the other way, as far as it can go the other way … And round again … and again.

I can feel a hand – your finger and thumb, surrounding me at the bottom of my penis. Your lips are taking me in further as you move them down my penis towards your hand. And your wet tongue is rubbing, sliding against my frenulum as you move further down.

I feel your lips squeezing me as you slide back up ... surrounding my penis but not squeezing it when you move back down ... pressing your tongue firmly against my shaft as you go up and stroking me as you go down.

Now your hand is rising with your lips, your finger and thumb just below your lips, holding and squeezing me as you move up, sliding over me on the way down.

I feel your lips and hand and tongue continuously moving up and down me in unison, wetting and palpating me. Up and down ... up and down.

...

Why did you stop?

I could taste your pre-come; it seeped out from your sex. I really want you to come inside me instead.

Perhaps, maybe, I want to taste your sex before that.

You can.

If you lie down and part your legs, then I can have access to you.

...

Don't you want to sit between my legs?

Yes, but you will need to raise your legs.

My knees are bent now.

Put your left leg over my right shoulder.

Like this.

Yes … Now close your eyes.

…

Your right hand is running through my outer left thigh, rolling the muscles forward … and backwards now … The other hand is stroking me inside my other thigh … I can feel the side of your face pressing against my left knee, submerging, moving inside as you stroke your cheek against it. Your eyes, nose and jaw sink into my knee as you twist to kiss my thigh. I feel your left hand smoothing and rubbing the right side of my groin, back and forth, up and down. Your face has left my knee and now your tongue is dragging itself through my skin, riding over the muscles of my left inner thigh, surfing back up from where it started – warm, gentle hands following.

When you kiss me, I can feel your lips dissolve into me and then the pull of your lips as you release… Another kiss … and another … approaching my sex … First on one thigh then doing it all again on the other thigh.

I feel your nose over my sex, brushing my labia, side to side, teasing them. I can feel the nerves setting themselves alight.

Now your tongue is running along the edge of my right outer labia … Over the hood of my clitoris and down the other outer labia. Your tongue is submerging itself at the bottom of my left outer labia, driving its way up and parting the upper-facing surface of it. It closes up behind as your tongue passes through it, just like water closing behind your hand as you move through it … All the way

230

to the top of the labia ... and now letting go of it ... You are doing the same to the right labia, starting from the bottom and working upwards.

I can feel your tongue now, between my vulva and my anus. You're pressing your tongue against me there ... It feels like your tongue has penetrated my body, entered it there, dived in, pointing inward ... mmm .... I feel your tongue inside me, moving upwards, from below my vulva, passing through the base of my vulva to the underside of my vagina ... ever upwards, as you try to pierce it and move inside it ... through my vagina, either side of your tongue touching the internal walls as you pass through, and now to the top of my vagina, lifting the upper wall as you seek your exit, parting me again as you move your tongue towards my clitoris ...

It's sensational!

...

I can feel your fingers pulling back the prepuce over my clitoris ... your finger squeezing it in a rhythmic manner.

Now your lips surrounding my clitoris ... Your tongue teasing it – flicking, pressing, rolling ...

I can feel a finger rimming my vagina, first one way then the other ... Your fingers slipping in.

The sucking motion of your lips on my clit is in harmony with your fingers slipping up and down the inside wall of my vagina ... With every sucking motion, you are working your way around the walls of my vagina, like the second hand on a clock.

...

You've released my clitoris!

I need to move to one side of you ... I'm going to continue to finger you, so keep your eyes closed. Put your legs down ... that's it ... Let me lean over. What do you feel now?

Your fingers have left my vagina and are holding onto the lower end of my inner lips ... I can feel the other hand grabbing the top end of the lips ... You're stretching me.

When I stretch you, my fingers and thumb sink into your labia.

Yes, I can feel it.

When I'm squeezing and stretching, my fingers merge with your lips, as if they are a part of them – extending your lips, making them seem longer, with my fingers ... and I can see that your vulva is engorged again and has deepened in colour.

I can see your sex. It has also has deepened in colour, and it's become more bulbous ... I'm just going to reach out and grab hold of your sex.

Close your eyes again.

Okay.

I can feel your hand around my penis, moving up and down it.

Now I feel your lips brushing my inner labia whilst your fingers are holding them at either end ... downwards and upwards, as you move your head side to side ...

Your lips take hold of my stretched inner labia, surrounding them ... And your tongue is sailing around the outside of them ... first one way then the other ... and again.

I can feel you pulling my labia upward and outwards into your mouth, with the suction of your kisses – I feel the soft tugging action.

Now your tongue is parting my squeezed labia. It feels like a wave rushing through my sex ... just like the wave of my hands travelling back and forth along your sex.

Your tongue is sensuous. But I need you to stop now. I need you to stop.

I need you to stop too. Your hand is causing me to breathe deeper and I can't concentrate.

Enter me. Get on top of me and enter me. My body is ready ... Quick, get between my legs ... Are you in?

You need to raise and widen your legs a bit more for me.

How about now?

That's better ... I am entering you.

Yes, I can feel you now.

I can feel the walls of your vagina surrounding me.

I can feel you parting me.

Your hands are on my backside.

Your face is next to mine – I can feel your cheek next to mine.

My arms are around you.

I can feel them around me, and your hips and pelvis are locking with mine.

Your breasts are pressing against me, entering my chest.

Your nipples have merged inside me. Our ribs are merging.

My body is sinking into yours.

I can feel your kiss on my neck.

I can feel your kiss on my shoulder.

You're pulling yourself out.

Your sex wants me to remain.

Your hips are loosening and freeing themselves.

Your hands: sinking into my backside.

Your body moving downwards.

Down through your ribs.

Your chest is tugging my breasts downwards.

Pulling away from your hips and pelvis.

I can feel your sex moving back in again.

It's listening to your hands, which have sunk into my backside, pushing me in.

Into my hips and pelvis again, upwards through my ribs and down again.

The walls of your sex.

The hardness of yours.

Your wetness.

Your thrusts.

Your heart is racing ... and so is mine.

I can feel your balls bashing against my body.

I can hear the squidgy noises as I go faster.

I can feel your sex touching my cervix as you thrust.

I can feel the tension of your muscles, in your stomach, in your pelvis, and in your sex muscles, as I thrust.

I can feel the tension of your muscles, too, as your body merges with mine.

Your hands are now on my back, holding me lightly. Your legs are around me, gripping me.

I think I'm nearly there.

…

*

I felt your sex pulse a few times in the last few thrusts. I could feel your semen ejaculate inside me.

I felt the whole of your sexual organs rhythmically contract – multiple times.

My whole pelvic region down to my anus contracted.

I felt some convulsions inside me from my pelvic region and then a rush of semen surging up through my sex, in multiple spasms.

I could feel the release in your lower back muscles when I was holding on to your back. I think your stomach muscles contracted just before mine. I remember feeling turned on as if your contractions were conducting me.

I felt the squeeze of your legs around my hips. Your vagina surrounded my sex during your contractions as if it wanted me to come.

And you did.

I also felt some of your "squirt" over my loins.

*

I like resting my head on you.

I like it when you are in my arms.

It's nice being with you here.

You. Me. The Voice.

Yes, the Voice that did not judge us.

You are right: our shared space was not judgemental.

…

It's nice when you caress my face and my forehead.

There is a certain stillness in this quietness.

It feels serene.

Even touching your face seems …

Nice?

Special.

Caresses are always special.

I like caressing your arms, too, and your back, and the leg which is lying across my body …

It feels like you are lulling me.

Into?

Your heart.

I just like the feel of you.

I like my hand resting upon your chest.

Give me your hand.

…

See what our hands look like together.

They look good together.

You are bringing our hands down now … to kiss them?

No, to smell them … Is this what my sex smells like?

That is the smell of your sex.

But?

But there was a slight smell of shit when I went down on you.

You're so romantic!

Ha ha! Sorry.

Smile again.

Hey!

Smile again ... Ha ha ha!

Don't laugh at my smile!

I'm not. You've got one of my pubic hairs in your teeth.

Oh.

Let me take it out.

...

You said I had some pre-come. What did that taste like?

I think I am leaking some of your semen.

I am dripping too.

Do you want to taste some?

No, I think I don't want to take that opportunity, just yet.

Anyway, I feel relaxed.

So do I!

Caress me some more ...

In a Café

I like it when we are sitting here drinking together.

I like it too.

I really don't think you feel comfortable being here.

Sometimes it is my quiet space. Other times, as you say, I feel uncomfortable. It's the same space but it seems to change meaning.

How so?

Did you see the drinks we got served?

Yes, why?

They were not made well. It is like that when I also order food.

How do you mean?

I get given what is not perfect, what has been left out on display longest, and often I get the least amount of what they serve, even though I know there are other servings available and I can see them being given to others. Things like this change the meaning of my space.

There seems to be less care given to me – people think that is what I deserve.

I did notice that the drinks were not perfect, but I did not notice you react.

I no longer react.

Why not?

It draws attention to me – I don't like the assault of people's gazes. Their gazes burn and bring a sense of stigma. The less I engage, the less time I am open to others, or, rather, am in front of others – the less hurt I can feel.

That woman behind the counter was not nice.

Did you see what happened?

Yes, I did.

What did you see?

I saw her customer-friendly smile disappear as you approached to be served. I heard no banter with you like she had with the previous customers and those that followed us. I saw her put your money down on the counter, when she was happily placing other people's money in their hands. I saw her talk to her colleagues whilst she glanced over to look in our direction after you were served – I had a feeling that we were the focus of her conversation.

Is that all you saw?

Perhaps the more I am with you, the more I will be able to see. But what I do see now is your head bowed and looking out the window, reluctant to observe life inside the café.

Do you see all those people around us talking and looking at us?

Yes, I do.

Do you see the people moving in our direction looking for a table, only to turn around and sit elsewhere once they caught a glimpse of me?

I know it is difficult for you.

Do you see the distance?

Yes, and it is not nice.

What else do you see?

I see their gazes.

Even though they may be talking about themselves, I cannot help thinking that they are talking about me. Their reality and my reality seem distorted.

Hold my hand.

…

I like sitting facing outwards looking through the window. The people outside are too busy in their lives to bother looking in; they do not usually stare into the café, they simply glance and scan to see how busy it is in here. And if one or two pairs of eyes do stare at me, I turn my head to look at the inside. The people inside the café who are not in conversation are here observing others and, on occasion, when I catch them looking at me, they see me trying to avoid looking at them – I do not want to become aware of who they are looking at.

Squeeze my hand … This is our space here right now. It is no longer about You and Them, but Us.

AUTHOR'S NOTES

Distortion was written as a challenge to my previous novel, *The Malady of Love* (*TMOL*). *TMOL* was an experimental piece, a dialogue-only text with no reference to time, place or person, using repetition to convey a sense of musicality in the dialogue, and contrasting this with some of the major themes. To describe hair colour, or a face, the character or the manner in which people communicate, would make the narrative less "portable" as it would fix these elements to the page. Thus, the reader was forced to focus on a narrative in which the "description" was in the emotional and psychological content of the characters' stories. The reader was therefore free to interpret all other (extraneous) elements for themselves, to make the characters more relatable.

The challenge in this novel became not that of the purely interior, but of the physical – to write a story that focused on two people who are physically different, and to avoid the internal angst, in its purest sense, of that situation as much as possible. Would this story of two "physically different" people be interesting enough for the reader?

The first thing to tackle was what the physical differences were going to be. The initial position was that there would be two "bodily different" people. But I felt that there was another perspective in being different to explore – one had to be visibly or facially different, as opposed to bodily different.

Next was to identify what the differences would be. A documentary alerted me to a condition called scoliosis, where, in the simplest sense, an individual develops a curvature of the spine. Research indicated that the prevalence of this was higher in females, and that a particular form, adolescent idiopathic scoliosis, develops from youth: that is, it becomes an acquired change with the onset of puberty, or around that time. My thoughts then led me to the male character. If her story was about an acquired difference, then his must be about one from birth, a congenital issue, as I wanted to differentiate between those who have experienced life not knowing anything else apart from their difference, and those who have known a life, to some extent, without difference, who then become different. Documentaries have tended to focus on those with facial differences being male; so I had to include that in the story. I also wanted to ensure that this was not about who had it "worse" than the other – acquired versus congenital issues – as this was not to be about competing difficulties.

The first principle for me was that those with differences were not going to be portrayed negatively; that is, as perpetrators or monsters. Look at the many stories out there where someone's physical difference is seen as evil: Shakespeare's Richard III, who, incidentally, is suspected to have had scoliosis; the many movies – horror, crime, et cetera, in which the perpetrators are facially different; television and newspapers that rarely illustrate those with a difference as being normal, and pat themselves on the back for having one episode or a single feature about an individual with a difference, on the pretext of being inclusive.

This principle happily restricted the story line, as thoughts regarding physical and visceral elements led to societal attitudes about body horror. For me, the bodies could not be portrayed as horrific. Subsequently, and thinking of a physical conflict as opposed to a psychological or emotional one, thoughts led me to examine violence to the body? But these characters were never going to be perpetrators so that simpletons could associate their physical difference with badness or wickedness.

The idea of body swap occurred to me, whereby the characters either wake up in each other's bodies or have been swapped whilst trying on the other character's body and are unable to escape from this new condition – they became stuck in their new clothing. In both cases, they would be disgusted with the idea of being in another different body, especially after what they had endured in life. Once again, my aim was not to achieve the effects of horror, nor to infer that "differences" are disgusting, but respect.

I stuck to the principle in *TMOL* that it was something within the relationship that caused the central challenge. Inevitably, the long-term isolation and alienation of the male character and the rejection of the female character would result in ongoing intimacy issues. Just to make it clear, those without physical differences also have intimacy issues, and those who are physically different can have no intimacy issues. In my research, it seemed that people's perception of those with physical differences tended to exclude their sexuality. It's like the idea that those with learning difficulties cannot have ordinary human needs, i.e. there is very often an absence of humanity in people's perception, and also in failing to empower individuals to express a full sense of their individual selves.

In exploring the sexuality issue, my research led me to look at such conditions as hyposexuality, sexual aversion, vaginismus, frigidity, et cetera, as conditions that needed to be overcome. The idea was for the characters to be guided through "therapy" to overcome their conditions. While sex therapy was seen as an ideal tool to overcome their issues there would have to be a lot of introspection – which was not the challenge for this story. However, sensate focus therapy could be included.

Sensate focus therapy is a set of structured behavioural techniques that help couples reduce negativity, anxiety and fear, without an emphasis on performance in intimacy, and to help communication. The stages include: non-demand touching, of self and partner; mutual touching; mutual touching with genital-to-genital contact and no insertion; mutual touching with genital-to-genital contact with insertion.

The initial intention here was to have the story as a chapter per sensate focus stage. But decided against it as there would need to be a lot of psychological, emotional disclosure after each stage or task was completed.

This is their journey, which for the reader starts at a point where the characters are together and want intimacy: no preamble, no description of how they got together, we just know that they are together at this point in time. And as with many couples, differences of opinion emerge when they think they are ready for something only to realise that they may not be.

They are naked, except for a sheet for modesty. Their bodies are laid bare, producing greater emphasis on them. They are at a distance from one another and express this through their words: neither sees each other's physical differences yet both describe them as they see them. The distance between them is also in their descriptions of each other: the river meanders or does not meander; deformity versus no deformity; hideousness versus beauty; perfection versus abnormality; natural disaster versus natural beauty. We are not sure if it is a form of denial or genuine perception. At least it hints at an early concept of distortion, whether it is the perception is of others or of themselves. Common ground is reached in their understanding of what tragedy and pain is. The distance lies in their opposing views and the slight artificiality of language, similar to people's early performances when getting to know someone.

The section "Against a Wall" perseveres with this distance, but to a lesser extent. The past is in the distance, but the present, the here and now, is written on their bodies. There is almost a disbelief about their pasts. There is a distance to the past, yet there is no distance, a zero distance, as they feel the eyes and gazes of others upon themselves. Their common ground is the pain and torture of operations endured, revealed through anaesthetic awareness. There is very little distance between their medical sufferings – "we had to be disfigured to correct our disfigurement". With a sense of guilt and shame, they perceive that they are responsible for ruining their parents' lives – they feel responsible for their impact on other people's lives while talking about how others have impacted them.

In coming to understand each other's medical sufferings, there still lingers a sense of distance through of the issue of understanding shame. But it is here, in "On the Floor", where the distances collapse between the world out there and the world inside, where the body becomes an embedded brace, where a face becomes an integral mask; where the teasing outside leads to internal destruction; where other people's gazes/laughter/actions penetrate internally. Here the brace and mask become an encroachment, an encasement, an entrapment, a protective layer to avoid the distance of endless exposure to others, via photographs, and other people's avoidant behaviour – ultimately resulting in a temporal distance: for her, her future identity is destroyed through the growth of her body; for him, the experience of suggested rejection at birth – something ingrained from way back. Distance that is now embedded and covering pain.

This chapter is about how the outside world ends up controlling the individual. There are constant references to societal and political themes: violating other people's norms; being rejected by society; criminality associated with those who are not beautiful, and beautiful persons being victims; how criminals, by association to perceived ugliness, should not be allowed to procreate; how past lives justify people's "lot in life" – an internal justification for their suffering – condemned from the outside, condemned from the inside. The concept of not allowing genes to be passed down through the generations emerges as the blaming of the mother for passing on or inheriting the genes.

The only way to overcome or to understand their anxiety is to disengage the embodied brace and mask. Through pain, there is freedom. And here we experienced the onion-peeling session. To avoid this being a psychological or emotional catharsis, it had to be demonstrated with the principle of the physical – the use of the body in torture: being stretched as on a rack; the use of machetes; face- or mask-ripping. Peeling back the layers via symbolic physical pain creates a space between what is clinging onto them and a desired future state – being free from those enforcements, having a breathing space, a space to be in.

Ultimately, their journey in these pages is one of closing the distance between themselves. Their common goals are achieved.

It should be noted that the concept of linking a broken, disfigured lip with the appearance of a vulva or vagina was derived from a theory in *The Science of Kissing* (Kirshenbaum, 2011) – "complex connection between color vision, sexual desire and the evolution of human life". In evolutionary terms, early man foraged for foods displaying a "superior ability to detect reddish color, giving them the advantage of locating the ripest fruits, which in turn helped them survive long enough to pass on their color detecting genes". As ancestors became primed to seek red food rewards, "they were probably going to check out the source of color wherever it occurred – including parts of the female anatomy ... It became emphasised on their bodies and in particular the labial region, serving to indicate a female's peak in fertility ... As ancestors stood upright, their bodies underwent many associated changes in response, including a shift in location of sexual signals ... our lips are quite literally a 'genital echo' ... resembling the female labia". If one set of lips becomes associated with stigma and hatred then what would happen if the other set of lips is found to have the same associations? Hence, very often, apprehensive or avoidant behaviour of the male character.

"In a Strange Place" describes the impact and aftermath of going through trauma, in this case their healthy "unravelling". The description had to be demonstrated behaviourally rather than emotionally via disturbance of sleep: anxiety preventing one from sleeping and anxiety while sleeping (in the form of night terrors or nightmare). For him, a Cubist self-image that collapses the face, indicating the fading of masks and the letting go of past issues. For her, psychosomatic associations with internal anxiety manifesting in bodily sensations and sweating.

"In a Candlelit Room" seeks to touch upon observational exploration towards becoming intimate – some distance to zero distance. This chapter tries to encapsulate all the stages of sensate therapy, with the use of artistic licence.

It was important in this part of their journey to set the scene for what was about to happen – unconditional touch, off-limit zones, safe words, touching to help the other rather than self-satisfaction, non-judgemental touching. Indeed, a dilemma was posed here about how to convert a behavioural approach into a dialogue-only one. I decided that dialogue had to be expressed, describing what was being undertaken, so that each could understand that the other knew the meaning, via observation, of what they were doing. Normally, one would not be so verbose during sensate therapy.

As sensate therapy progresses, the couple moves towards greater intimacy. So, the reader finds themselves forgetting the outside world and sharing the space with the characters. By the very nature of intimacy, it is a private space in relation to one and another. The distance for the characters is closing ("The shape of our bodies did not exist") and the reader is reducing their own distance to the actors by being immersed progressively. The exploration of the bodies through touch means that we focus on the touching and on what is being touched, removing the observational gaze upon physically different bodies in favour of one that the reader can relate to – a body, our body, that can be touched. We, like the characters, begin to shift our relationship to their bodies. While the reader has a choice to not read any further, their perseverance renders the reader a voyeur of the growing intimacy.

This leads us to "In a Shared Space". Where once the actors were at a distance, whether observational, temporal, experiential, fear-inducing, they are now in the here and now with no sociological, political, philosophical or historical considerations and only a casual reminder of their landscapes, as you would expect when talking about intimacy. The flow of their philosophical musings weaving in and out of their dialogue now becomes the physical flow of their bodies – the weaving into and out of their visceral selves.

Sharing a space with another voice is a technique used to describe things that normally, in intimacy, voices would not be doing. Connecting to a third voice is equating to a third body (a concept derived from Hélène Cixous's *The Third Body*) or the sense of others having to look in. In this case, their own voices are looking at themselves, to comfort them, informing them that an inward gaze, albeit their own, is not always threatening or negative but can simply be a descriptive one that tells "as is", without a distorted lens.

This chapter uses four stages of human sexual response: Excitement, Plateau, Orgasm, Resolution. As one progresses through the chapter, the couple are guided through these stages. There are also references to *The Science of Kissing* (Kirshenbaum, 2011) here, in talking about the human response to kissing: nerve impulses, hormone exchange in saliva, women closing eyes to judge males, the smell of the individual, pulse increasing, et cetera. Further references in this chapter are made to some techniques used in *Yoni Massage: Awakening Female Sexual Energy* (Riedle, 2009) and *Lingam Massage: Awakening Male Sexual Energy* (Riedle and Becker, 2010).

Here, in this chapter, the reader forgets about the world around them and focuses on the private acts of intimacy being undertaken. The reader is as immersed in the dialogue as the characters are physically.

"In a Café" is a timely reminder that whatever journey the couple might take, to whatever level of intimacy there might be between them, they live in the context of an outside world. Their resolution is not the resolution of the world. The context is of reality, not only for the characters, but for the reader as well – the understanding that these characters live in the wider world, an unforgiving world.

Sierra Ernesto Xavier, 2022

Acknowledgements

The following materials were used as background reading and I wish to thank the authors for their inspiration.

<u>Books</u>

Baughan, R. (2008) *The Butterfly Girl.* London: John Blake Publishing Limited

Blume, J. (2001) *Deenie.* Lincoln: Macmillan Children's books

Cixous, H. (1999) *The Third Body.* US: Northwestern University Press

Davidow, J. (2003) *Marked For Life: A Memoir.* New York: Harmony Books

Di Prima, D. (1998) *Memoirs of a Beatnik.* New York: Penguin Books

Grealy, L. (1994) *Autobiography of a Face.* New York: Houghton Mifllin Company

Halberstam-Mickel, I. (1989) *Stand Up Straight: Personal Recollections About Scoliosis By People Who Live With It.* Iowa: Kendall/Hunt Publishing Company

Harris, M. and Hunt, N. (eds) (2008) *Fundamentals of Orthognathic Surgery.* London: Imperial College Press

Kaplan, H.S. (1987) *The Illustrated Manual of Sex Therapy 2nd Edition.* New York: Routledge

Kirshenbaum, S. (2011) *The Science of kissing: What Our Lips Are Telling Us.* New York: Grand Central Publishing

Leduc, V. (1972) *The Taxi.* Farrar, Straus & Giroux

Marsden, J. (2004) *So Much To Tell You.* London: Walker Books

Neuwirth, M. and Osborn, K. (2001) *The Scoliosis Sourcebook.* New York: Contemporary Books

Papel, Ira D. et al. (eds) (2009) *Facial and Plastic Reconstructive Surgery 3rd Edition.* Thieme Medical Publishers

Rakes, A. (2006) *Plastic Back.* Lincoln: iUniverse

Riedle, M. (2009) *Yoni Massage: Awakening Female Sexual Energy.* Vermont: Destiny Books

Riedle, M. and Becker, J. (2010) *Lingam Massage: Awakening Male Sexual Energy.* Vermont: Destiny Books

Rumsey, N. and Harcourt, D. (2005) *The Psychology of Appearance.* England: Open University Press

Sohrabi, L. (1983) *The Crooked Journey: The Story of a Woman's Fight Against Scoliosis.* Alameda, CA: Rima Press

Spray, M. (2002) *Growing Up With Scoliosis: A Young Girl's Story.* USA: Stratford, Conneticut

Trust, D. (1987) *Overcoming Disfigurement.* Northamptonshire: Thorsons Publicity Group

Weiner, L. and Avery-Clark, C. (2017) *Sensate Focus in Sex Therapy: The Illustrated Manual.* New York: Routledge

Wolpert, D.K. (2005) *Scoliosis Surgery: The Definitive Patient's Reference (2nd ed.).* US: Swordfish Communications

Zephaniah, B. (2003) *Face.* London: Bloomsbury

Articles

Blitz, A. and Sklenar, D. (2004) *Facial Difference: Beyond The Medical Issues*. Journal of Cranial Facial Surgery (2004) 15, 4, July 2004.

Buchanan, E.P. and Hyman, C.H. (2013) *LeFort 1 Osteotomy*. Seminars in Plastic Surgery 2013; 27: 149–154.

Bonilla Carrasco, M.I. and Solano Ruiz, M.C. *Perceived Self-image in Adolescent Idiopathic Scoliosis: An Integrative Review of the Literature*. Rev. Esc. Enferm. USP 2014, 48, 748–757.

Durmala, J; Blicharska, I; Drosdzol-Cop, A.; Skrzypulec-Plinta, V. (2014) *The assessment of the sexual functioning in women with idiopathic scoliosis - preliminary study*. Scoliosis 2014, 9(Supplement 1): O82.

Heather C. Trepal-Wollenzier MEd & Kelly L. Wester MA (2002) *The Use of Masks in Counselling*. Journal of Clinical Activities, Assignments & Handouts in Psychotherapy Practice, 2:2, 123–130.

Horton, K.M.; Renooy, L.; Forrest, C.R. (2000) *Patients with Facial Difference: Assessment of Information and Psychosocial Support Needs*. University of Toronto Medical Journal (2000) 78, 1, 8–11.

Millstone, S. (2008) *Coping with Disfigurement 1: Causes and Effects*. Nursing Times; 104: 12, 26–27.

Moss, T.P. (2005) *The Relationships between Objective and Subjective ratings of Disfigurement Severity, and Psychological Adjustment*. Body Image 2 (2005) 151–159.

Newell, R. and Marks, I. (2000) Phobic Nature of Social Difficulty in Facially Disfigured People. British Journal of Psychiatry (2000), 176, 177–181.

Ólafsson, Y.; Saraste, H; Ahlgren, R-M. (1999) *Does Bracing Affect Self-Image? A prospective study on 54 patients with adolescent idiopathic scoliosis.* European Spine Journal (1999) 8:402–405.

Olver, J.M. (2000) *Raising the Suborbicularis Oculi Fat (SOOF): Its role in Chronic Facial Palsy.* British Journal of Opthamology 2000; 84:1401-1406.

Schroeder, J. E.; Michaeli, T.; Luria, M.; Barzilay, Y.; Hasharoni, A.; Kaplan, L. (2012) *The Effect of Scoliosis Correction on Sexual Function of Women with Adolescent Idiopathic Scoliosis.* Global Spine Journal 2012; 02–P22.

Internet Resources

Changing Faces
https://www.changingfaces.org.uk

Cornell Health (2019) Sensate Focus – Article
https://health.cornell.edu/

The Marital Intimacy Institute
https://maritalintimacyinst.com/

The Rhinoplasty Center
https://www.therhinoplastycenter.com/

Treating Scoliosis
https://www.treatingscoliosis.com

Ussin-Davey, A. (2003) Disfigurement, sexuality issues can be addressed

https://billingsgazette.com/lifestyles/health-med-fit/disfigurement-sexuality-issues-can-be-addressed/article_ff72da63-afc5-5798-8839-60f4e374b1aa.html

Whitefield-Madrano, A. (2012) What Scoliosis Taught Me About Body Image
https://www.huffpost.com/entry/scoliosis-body-image_b_1402822